SAVING SIENNA

MACARTHUR FAMILY SERIES

Katie Reus

Cover art: Jaycee of Sweet 'N Spicy Designs
Editor: Julia Ganis
Author website: https://www.katiereus.com

Saving Sienna/Katie Reus. -- 1st ed.
KR Press, LLC

ISBN 13: 9781635561562

eISBN: 9781635561555

For misfits everywhere.

Praise for the novels of Katie Reus

"...a wild hot ride for readers. The story grabs you and doesn't let go."
—*New York Times* bestselling author, Cynthia Eden

"Has all the right ingredients: a hot couple, evil villains, and a killer action-filled plot. . . . [The] Moon Shifter series is what I call Grade-A entertainment!" —Joyfully Reviewed

"I could not put this book down. . . . Let me be clear that I am not saying that this was a good book *for* a paranormal genre; it was an excellent romance read, *period.*" —All About Romance

"Reus strikes just the right balance of steamy sexual tension and nail-biting action....This romantic thriller reliably hits every note that fans of the genre will expect." —*Publishers Weekly*

"Prepare yourself for the start of a great new series! . . . I'm excited about reading more about this great group of characters."
—Fresh Fiction

"Wow! This powerful, passionate hero sizzles with sheer deliciousness. I loved every sexy twist of this fun & exhilarating tale. Katie Reus delivers!" —Carolyn Crane, RITA award winning author

"A sexy, well-crafted paranormal romance that succeeds with smart characters and creative world building." —Kirkus Reviews

"*Mating Instinct*'s romance is taut and passionate . . . Katie Reus's newest installment in her Moon Shifter series will leave readers breathless!"
—Stephanie Tyler, *New York Times* bestselling author

"You'll fall in love with Katie's heroes."
—*New York Times* bestselling author, Kaylea Cross

"Both romantic and suspenseful, a fast-paced sexy book full of high stakes action." —Heroes and Heartbreakers

"Katie Reus pulls the reader into a story line of second chances, betrayal, and the truth about forgotten lives and hidden pasts."
—The Reading Café

"Nonstop action, a solid plot, good pacing, and riveting suspense."
—RT Book Reviews

"Exciting in more ways than one, well-paced and smoothly written, I'd recommend *A Covert Affair* to any romantic suspense reader."
—Harlequin Junkie

"Sexy military romantic suspense." —USA Today

"Enough sexual tension to set the pages on fire."
—*New York Times* bestselling author, Alexandra Ivy

"*Avenger's Heat* hits the ground running...This is a story of strength, of partnership and healing, and it does it brilliantly."
—Vampire Book Club

"*Mating Instinct* was a great read with complex characters, serious political issues and a world I am looking forward to coming back to."
—All Things Urban Fantasy

PROLOGUE

Four months ago

Carson held on to Sienna's hips, holding her closer than necessary as they swayed to the music. This woman was pure fire in his arms, sensual, funny, and gorgeous.

His sister Kathryn had just gotten married and she and her new husband—Sienna's brother—had already left.

But the reception was in full swing and even though he'd planned on leaving early, he'd decided to stay as long as Sienna did. Because he couldn't seem to get enough of her.

"I've never seen you look so relaxed," Sienna said. She had a bunch of little flower things in her hair and had curled it so that it was around her face in waves, making her look like a fairy princess.

And the fact that he was thinking those words told him he'd probably had too much to drink. "I know how to have a good time," he murmured, his gaze falling to her mouth. Damn, he wanted to show *her* a good time. Wanted to get her off with his mouth, his fingers, hear her moan his name as she came...

She snorted softly.

He frowned. "What?"

"Nothing. You just always seem so serious."

For the most part he was. No use denying that. In the last couple weeks he'd learned that Sienna was most definitely not. They'd both been involved in the wedding—Daniel had surprisingly asked Carson to be a groomsman, and his sister had asked Sienna to be a bridesmaid, which was not a surprise. Those two were thick as thieves. And everyone seemed to like Sienna.

Himself included.

She always had a mischievous gleam in her eyes though, as if she was up to something. And he found himself ridiculously intrigued by her. He wanted to know every little thing about her, which disturbed him.

As the music stopped, she grabbed his hand and tugged him along with her without even asking.

Later, he would realize he hadn't even thought to protest, he'd just gone along. Because why wouldn't he? "Where are we going?" he asked as she continued off the dance floor and through the throng of tables. It was like the bride and groom had invited the whole town.

She flashed him a quick grin that lit up her whole face. "You'll see."

For a brief moment he wondered if she was going to drag them up to her hotel room. Even though it would likely be a mistake since they were sort of related now, he found he didn't care in the least. But no, she was taking them to the kitchen.

"Pretty sure you're not allowed in here," he said as she pushed through the swinging door to where the catering crew was moving about.

To his surprise, one of the servers smiled and gave her a little wave. "Hey, Sienna, you need anything?"

"No. Daniel said he left something for me."

The woman smiled and nodded and didn't question their presence at all.

Carson followed her to one of the walk-in refrigerators and couldn't help but stare as she bent over, her already tight-fitting dress pulling taut against the most perfect ass in the world as she bent down and grabbed...

She made a sound of pleasure as she pulled out a very expensive bottle of champagne and held it up. "Success!"

Carson lifted an eyebrow. He recognized the brand and it was like a month's salary for him. Probably more. "Your brother left that for you?"

She lifted a shoulder, that mischievous glint firmly in place. "Maybe not for me *exactly*, but he's already gone, so this is ours."

He shook his head slightly and, moving on instinct, he grabbed for her hip, tugging her to him. God, he wanted this woman more than he'd ever wanted anyone. She called to him on the most basic level.

She moved immediately against him, wrapping her arms around his neck, the bottle lying against his back as their mouths collided.

They'd been flirting on and off over the last week through all the wedding stuff, and deep down he knew they'd been building to this. Hopefully to more. Because she was the kind of woman you held on to and never let go.

She tasted sweet, like the cake they'd had earlier. And she felt like heaven in his arms, tall and lean, and she fit perfectly against him.

Suddenly the door opened and Sienna pulled back.

One of the servers he recognized from the kitchen stared at them wide-eyed. "Oh, ah, I'm sorry."

"No, we're sorry. We'll get out of your way." Then Sienna was moving again, tugging him along with her.

He wasn't used to being manhandled but he found he liked it when Sienna did it. He realized he was simply following her anywhere she dragged him and… He was surprisingly okay with that. She could manhandle him straight to the bedroom. Or shower. Or any flat surface really. He wanted her hands all over him.

As they hurried back into the kitchen, he grabbed two glasses from a drying rack.

She arched an eyebrow, her grin pure wicked. "You think I'm sharing with you?"

"I think if you drink a whole bottle by yourself, I'll be carrying you to your room."

She laughed as they exited the kitchen, the pure music of it wrapping around him, warming him from the inside out.

In that moment, he realized he could fall really hard and really fast for this woman.

CHAPTER ONE

Sienna snapped another picture of the interior of the expensively furnished stateroom on this ridiculous yacht. With each picture, her smile grew a little bit wider.

Some jerk thought he could hide his assets from his wife? That was where Sienna came in.

Snap. She snagged another picture of the paneled ceiling and track lighting. The wood was quality, a nice pale color that made the room seem even bigger. With four oversized windows, whoever stayed in this room would have a gorgeous ocean view from most angles.

She flipped to panorama mode and got everything in one swoop.

Snap.

Another one of the bathroom—which was nicer than hers at home. Two pedestal bowls over a white-and-gray marble countertop. The backsplash was intricate, the white and grays of the tile changing with each step she took, as if they were liquid. Whoever had designed this had an incredible eye—and money to burn. She took another panorama of this room too, wanting to get all of its glory.

As she stepped out into the wood-paneled passageway, she scrolled back through her pictures. Triumph surged through her as she scanned the gorgeous colors popping in each image. The sunlight really had been in her favor today and these images were going to help her client get everything she deserved in her divorce.

Sienna uploaded the photos to the cloud, then tucked her phone away, as well as her backup camera. Because she *always* had a backup.

As she headed in the direction of the aft deck, ready to disembark as soon as she could, she froze when she heard male voices.

Hell. She'd had to pay off someone at the marina to get access to this particular boat. The woman running the desk for some of the rental charters also headed up access for the cleaning crews. All it had taken was a hundred bucks and a bit of the truth about what she was doing and the woman had told her she had an hour to get in and out.

Sienna had only been here for twenty minutes, so clearly something had gone wrong.

Unfortunately she knew what she had to do.

Pulling her phone back out, she turned the volume down and tucked it and the small camera into her plastic waterproof case hooked around her neck by a sturdy lanyard. She'd brought this just in case, because as a private investigator, she *always* liked to be prepared.

And this wasn't the first time she'd had to find an alternate escape—by means of jumping over the side of a boat.

She picked up her pace as she hurried in the opposite direction along the wood-paneled passageway with wide, tinted windows overlooking the marina. Her heart skipped a beat as she spotted three men walking along the outer passageway, likely going in the direction of the flybridge. One of the men looked at her and... *Oh God!* Wait, he couldn't see her. Not with the tint. Still, her adrenaline surged.

Feeling bold, she pulled out her phone and snapped a few pictures of all three men without the flash. Actual images of her client's husband on this boat that he was pretending he didn't own? That was gold!

But now she had to hurry. She ducked out of sight and on silent feet she hurried through the kitchen. The voices got louder as she eased the other galley door open. It silently closed behind her, but her heart was an erratic drumbeat in her ears.

It wasn't like there were cameras here, and the owner was hiding that he even owned this yacht—in an attempt to screw his wife over in their divorce. Sienna didn't think he'd call the cops if he found her. If he did, he'd have to admit he owned it on the record.

Still, she did not relish getting caught. Because from everything she'd found out about this guy, he was not a nice person. He might try to hurt her as opposed to calling the authorities.

As she stepped into the open living area, she raced across it and opened the door that led to one of the outside decks. A blast of summer air hit her as she stepped outside. Just as quickly she shut the door behind her, trying to force her heartbeat to slow down.

The deck chairs were all stacked together, not set out as if they were about to be used. She glanced around the marina, saw everything was mostly quiet, though a few fishing boats were heading in.

These yachts were owned by people who rarely used their expensive toys—people who had more money than sense. Or common decency, in her experience.

She glanced around and knew she only had a minute or two max to escape without being discovered. Since she was on the bottom level, she didn't have far to go. Sighing, she hoisted herself over the edge of the railing and dropped down into the water.

She made a splash, there was no way around it.

Kicking off the side of the boat, she swam away from the bow toward another row of smaller boats—cruising sailboats. Her arms and legs burned as she swam, her shoes weighing her down. She risked a glance over her shoulder as she reached the next occupied boat slip. No one was shouting at her at least so maybe no one had seen her.

Of course there could be any number of people watching her from one of the yacht's interior rooms. Oh well, she couldn't help it now.

She just needed to get onto dry land—and get out of here fast.

Heart racing as she swam around the nearest sailboat and toward a sturdy-looking ladder, she kicked harder. As she reached the top, two strong hands grabbed her under the armpits, hauling her up.

She started to struggle, going into pure fight mode until she realized who it was. "Crap," she muttered. What the hell was *he* doing here?

Carson Irish, brother to her new sister-in-law. A sexy detective she'd fooled around with once. Or twice... Gah, three times! A man she couldn't get out of her head. His gaze swept the length of her dripping wet body, then he looked up and down the dock and sighed.

Across from them a shrimper eyed them for about a second, then went back to work untangling his net. Clearly he didn't care what they were up to, which was good for her.

"Can we get the hell out of here?" she finally said, her adrenaline still pumping. The sailboat blocked them from view of the yacht, but she needed to get out of these wet clothes, check her phone and camera, and she really, *really* wanted to put as much distance as possible between her and the men on the yacht.

Jaw tight, Carson simply held on to her elbow as if he thought she'd run from him and they hurried down the dock toward the parking lot.

"Why are you here anyway? Are you following me?" she muttered as they reached the gravel parking lot, her sneakers making squishing sounds with each step.

"Where are you parked?" he asked instead of actually answering as they reached his truck.

"Over there," she said, jerking her chin and trying to hold on to some sliver of dignity even as water pooled around her feet and her clothes stuck to her in odd places. She really hated that she was wearing a white T-shirt and a bralette right about now.

"Follow me to my place," he said—basically ordered. "You can dry off there."

She had a change of clothes and a towel in her trunk, but she wanted to grill him more about what he was doing here. "Thanks," she murmured before jogging off to her Jeep. As her clothing made weird sucking sounds against her body, she realized that she'd been a fool for hoping for any sort of dignity at this point.

Sienna had been to Carson's place before—once—so she knew exactly how to get there. He lived in a low-rise, two-bedroom condo two blocks from the beach. It was nice, with more than decent security, and since she knew where his assigned parking spot was, she parked there instead of in guest parking. By the time she grabbed her duffel bag out of the back of her Jeep and made it to his front door, he'd joined her on the front step.

"You mind stripping off before you come inside?" There was a hint of challenge in his voice, and in those pale blue eyes she wanted to drown in.

If he thought she wasn't up to it, he was very wrong. As he headed inside, she left her shoes outside on his mat and stripped off everything except her bralette, panties and the lanyard around her neck. She'd checked on her phone and camera and they had come through her adventure perfectly fine.

When he returned a few moments later, his eyes widened slightly as his gaze swept over her shivering body, but he handed her a towel and, to her surprise, glanced away as if trying not to stare.

Which was just as well. They'd tried to make something work a few months ago and it simply hadn't happened. Okay, that was a huge lie. She'd run away when he'd tried to get serious, because that was what she always did. Men were more hassle than anything. Except...that wasn't true with Carson.

"Think I could grab a quick shower?" she asked through chattering teeth as she tightened the towel around her.

"Yes." He looked at her, his expression unreadable. "Then you and I are going to talk."

That sounded ominous so she chose to ignore his words. She plucked her bag up and headed to the guest bathroom instead of his. It would feel too intimate, too weird to take a shower in his.

She didn't want to see where he kept all his personal things or know if he hung his towel up after showering. *Nope, nope, nope.* That was more information than she needed in her head. Especially since she knew exactly how he sounded and looked when he climaxed. She'd been doing her best to ignore that she still wanted him with a hungry desperation bordering on stupid. It was like she couldn't just shut her brain off, couldn't completely forget about him—about his wicked kisses and all the dirty things he'd murmured in her ear.

By the time she'd washed the ocean out of her hair and gotten dressed, she felt like a new person. She even had mascara in her duffel bag so she swiped some on for good measure. And that was going to be the only makeup she had for the rest of the day, which was just as well.

She had jeans, a T-shirt and flip-flops in her duffel bag, which was perfect for today. After braiding her damp hair, she found Carson in his kitchen, leaning against one of the countertops, his phone in hand as he looked at something.

His hair was cropped close to his head, showing off perfect bone structure. Even the bit of dark scruff on his face looked sexy instead of unkempt. His T-shirt molded to all of his muscles, particularly his biceps, which she'd had fantasies about. At five feet eleven, she was used to being taller than a lot of men, but with Carson she actually had to look up. He had to be at least six feet four inches. Maybe five. And he was built like...well, like someone she wanted to wrap her legs around.

He immediately tucked his phone into his back pocket when he spotted her. His eyes heated for a moment as he took in her appearance. "I wondered what happened to that T-shirt."

She was wearing one of his faded black and white Ramones T-shirts, had tied it at her waist because it was way too big. "I'm not giving it back."

"I didn't ask for it."

She sniffed once and looked away, glancing around his kitchen. Everything was all neat and tidy, no surprise. This man liked order in his life. And she was like a wrecking ball.

"I tossed your sneakers and your clothes into the washer."

Surprised, she looked back at him. "Thanks. So were you following me?" she asked bluntly, wanting to get that out of the way now.

"Not exactly. But I saw you sneaking around so I decided to hang out and see what you were up to. Then I watched you break into a multimillion-dollar yacht."

"I didn't break into anything." The sliding door had been unlocked.

He lifted a dark eyebrow. "Fine, I watched you bribe someone and then get onto the boat."

"So you're kind of stalking me, then? Pretty sure that's against the law."

Carson's mouth curved up slightly at the corners, making him look ridiculously adorable. Such a big, bulky guy should not be adorable. "So is breaking and entering."

"I already told you, there was no breaking. Just entering. And technically, that yacht should be part of my clients' asset list. Her husband just forgot to add it to their divorce proceedings."

"I figured as much," he said mildly.

"Did you happen to see who got on the yacht while I was on it?" She'd seen three men, but wondered if there had been more.

"Just three guys. I was more concerned with making sure you got off safely than who they were. I was pretty close to making an excuse and going aboard."

She blinked in surprise. "Seriously?"

"*Seriously*. Trouble seems to find you."

She made a scoffing sound and pulled her thankfully dry phone out of her pocket. Her entire life was in her phone. "I've gotta go," she said as she read her incoming text message.

"Everything okay?" He pushed off the countertop, going into what she thought of as sexy mode. He had on a T-shirt and jeans, and his badge and gun weren't visible. Maybe he'd left them in his car or put them away. He didn't look anything like a detective right now. No, he looked more like a street brawler with his tattoos and scruff.

"Everything's fine. I just need to go see a client about something."

"You need to be more careful," he said as she headed for the door, duffel bag tossed over her shoulder.

"Last time I checked, I don't answer to you."

His gaze fell on her mouth, lingered too long as he met her at the door. He stood in front of it for a long moment, blocking her way. "You drive me crazy and I still want to kiss you right now," he murmured.

Why, oh why, did he always just say whatever was on his mind? It simultaneously drove her crazy and was also sort of hot. Well, not sort of. It was super hot. Just like the man himself.

She let out a growl of frustration and nudged him out of the way.

But he decided to follow her outside, carrying another towel with him. "Take this to dry off your seat."

Dang it, why was he so thoughtful? Because her seat was definitely still wet even with the towel she'd sat on.

"Thanks...ah, I can pick my clothes up later, I guess?"

"I'll get them to you. I can drop them off at your place."

"Okay, thanks. Just text me," she said as she slid into the front seat and rolled down her window, glad for a bit of a barrier between them.

"Are you actually going to text me back this time?" He leaned on the top of the frame, looking at her through the open window.

She tried not to obsess over the way his forearms and biceps flexed, or stare at the plethora of tattoos winding around said biceps and disappearing under the sleeves of his T-shirt. Some had to do with his military days, others were Celtic designs linked to his Irish heritage. Each one meant something, she knew. "I'll text you back about my clothes."

"But not about anything else, huh?" Again, his tone was dry.

"Not if you're going to ask me out on another date."

His gaze landed on her mouth again and heat rushed through her, wild and hungry. For him. It took all of her self-control not to whip her door open and devour him. Just climb him like a tree and have her way with him.

This man was her kryptonite and she was determined to stay away from him. She knew how good he tasted, how talented he was with that mouth, and she had so little control right now. So she started rolling the window up, which just made him laugh as he stood up. For some reason she always seemed to amuse him.

Meanwhile he drove her absolutely insane. Whenever she was around him, she wanted to crawl out of her skin he had her wound so tight.

Because getting involved with Carson Irish again? Absolutely no way in hell. That way would lead to heart-break.

CHAPTER TWO

Sienna sat down in front of Eileen Bentley's desk and spread out the blown-up pictures of the yacht. She'd already sent them directly to her client, but she could admit that she liked to be a bit of a showman on occasion. Especially when she'd taken such gorgeous pictures.

After leaving Carson this morning, she'd stopped by the hospital to see a client—and had run into her brother Brodie, who was apparently smitten with someone—and she'd been running around all day ever since.

"These are incredible," Eileen said, touching the photos. She shook her head slightly. "I can't believe he thought he could hide this from me. That he thought I'd be so stupid."

"That's not all he's hiding," she said. Because Sienna hadn't set up this meeting just to show her client the printed pictures. She pulled out another file and set it on the desk. "He's hiding money in various accounts as well. A hundred thousand here, another hundred thousand there."

Eileen's expression darkened as she flipped open the file and briefly scanned the first page. The woman had given up her career for her husband, and they didn't have kids. But her husband had wanted her to be a stay-at-home wife, to take care of everything for him, set up business dinners, organize his multiple businesses in an admin capacity. She'd basically been working for him for free as an executive assistant. And Eileen had been very good at her job. She'd saved her husband from a couple lawsuits and had organized two of his restaurants so much they'd nearly doubled earnings in one year.

Sienna saw that a lot, wives giving away all their labor for free and then, in the end, their husbands tossed them over as if they meant nothing. She could admit that it enraged her and she liked helping all these women get what they deserved.

Because that kind of shit would affect Eileen's Social Security down the line, or make her less hirable, something that a lot of people, especially women, didn't think about.

Sienna kept those thoughts to herself, however. Because at this point, Eileen was going to come out of the other side of this divorce in very good shape.

"If he's smart, he'll skip court altogether so none of this becomes public, and you guys should be able to work out an agreement," Sienna added.

Eileen's expression was still dark and when she smiled it was more of a baring of teeth. "Oh, he'll come to an agreement."

It seemed her work here was done. Sienna stood and held out a hand. "Sorry you're dealing with all this, but I hope you're able to settle quickly and move on with your life."

"Thank you," Eileen said as she stood as well, offering a perfectly manicured hand. "Hiring you was the best thing my lawyer ever advised me to do."

After leaving, Sienna decided to stop and grab a beer and a bunch of fried food before going home. She didn't have anything in her refrigerator, and after the day she'd had, she was starving.

As she slid onto a barstool at a local burger joint she'd only recently discovered, she nodded once at the bartender. Thankfully they weren't too busy tonight. "Cheeseburger with fried onion rings and a Guinness," she said.

"Make it two." Carson freaking Irish, like a ghost who came out of nowhere, sat next to her.

She was secure in her observational skills, but damn, she hadn't even seen him come in. She blinked at him. "Seriously, stalk much?"

"I swear I didn't know you were going to be here. I was back at that booth and saw you walk in. Besides, I'm the one who introduced you to this place."

Sienna bit back a reply because Carson was right. Maybe she'd subconsciously come here because she'd wanted to see him? No, she refused to believe that. She was simply hungry. *For food.* "Did you just get off work?"

He nodded and she realized he looked exhausted, so she decided not to needle him. Much.

"Rough day?" she continued.

He scrubbed a hand over his face and took the beer placed in front of him with a nod of appreciation. "You could say that."

"Want to talk about it?" She wrapped her fingers around her Guinness, letting it settle in its frosted mug as she traced her finger from the top of the glass to the bottom.

"Not really. How about you? Did your day get better?" There was definitely a hint of amusement in his tone now.

"Well, I didn't have to jump into any more bodies of water, so I call that a win. Plus...I'm pretty sure my brother has fallen for someone." Seeing Brodie all smitten had been a surprise.

Carson shot her a sharp glance.

"Not Daniel—he's obsessed with your sister. Something you know. You were at the freaking wedding."

He grinned then and it softened all of his hard features, making her panties melt just a little bit. She'd never understood the phrase panty-melting before Carson Irish.

"True," he said. "It's the only reason he's alive."

"I'm going to pretend you're just joking."

"I am. But there was a time when I wanted to punch his face in." Carson's expression went all surly for a moment.

"You and me both, but at least he got it together and married Kathryn." And now Sienna had a new sister. Another reason she wasn't going to play with fire, aka Carson. She didn't want to screw up their family dynamics.

"So what are you doing after this?"

"Going home, maybe a hot bath, then bed. I've got a lot of paperwork to do tomorrow. I never realized how much paperwork would be involved with being a PI."

He grinned and she really liked that look on him. "It's a lot more sitting in cars and waiting on stuff to happen than you thought, huh?"

She laughed lightly. "Yes. But I still love it. I like puzzles, mysteries—and I really like helping spouses uncover when their significant others are trying to hide stuff from them. It's just so shady and gross."

He nodded, watching her thoughtfully. "Did you have a bad breakup?"

She blinked at the abrupt personal question. "Why?"

"Not that I think I'm God's gift to women or anything, but you and I have chemistry. And don't deny it," he said when she opened her mouth to do just that. "Because I know you weren't faking with me. But you refuse to see if we can take it any further. Plus you take a whole lot of joy in 'sticking it to,' and I'm only quoting you, 'asshole men.'"

She took a sip of her beer, mulled over her response as a mournful Irish ballad played in the background. Finally she cleared her throat. "First, yes we have chemistry." So much. And no, she hadn't been faking her orgasms. So many orgasms. "Second...you're my sister-in-law's brother. That's way too messy and complicated." And those were two things Sienna did not deal with. They'd had sex, sure, but...yikes. More would not work. Nope.

There was more to it than that but she was so not going to give Carson the real reason.

Instead she continued, "And yes, I do enjoy sticking it to assholes. They deserve it. I like to believe I'm helping deal out a little cosmic karmic justice. It has nothing to do with any particular man or...whatever. I love my brothers. They're amazing. So is my dad. And so are a ton of other guys I know. I'm not a man-hater."

His gaze narrowed slightly. "What guys?"

She snorted softly as their burgers were placed in front of them. "Please tell me you're not jealous."

He lifted a shoulder. "Well, I'm certainly not going to lie to you."

She blinked at his words. "Are you always so honest?"

"With you." Carson watched her intently, his blue eyes vivid in the dim bar.

Damn it. He really did always say the right thing.

She looked away from him and down at her burger. It looked as if they'd added an extra slice of cheese. Her mouth watered. "I'm about to show you a good time," she said to her food, which made him throw his head back and laugh.

"I love that I never know what's going to come out of your sexy mouth," he murmured. Then he took a bite of his own burger.

She...didn't know how to respond to that. She did, however, like sitting there with him with the quiet buzz of the bar around them.

When she was with him, the silence was never uncomfortable. No, it was more companionable. He was content with just being with her too.

She swore he was like the perfect man for her.

Except...he didn't like her job. Didn't like that she got put in dangerous situations. And she wasn't going to change who she was for anyone.

Not even the sexiest man she'd ever known.

"Damn it," he muttered, breaking into her thoughts.

She looked over and saw him reading a message on his phone. "What's up?"

"We're shorthanded now, just got called out on something."

Sienna fought the disappointment that he had to leave. It wasn't like she'd planned to see him tonight anyway. That had just been a bonus she wouldn't admit to. "Stay safe," she murmured.

Giving her a look she couldn't even begin to describe, he tossed a few bills on the bar, more than covering both their meals. She wanted to protest, but knew it would be pointless.

As he headed out, an unexpected pang slid through her rib cage, hitting her right in the heart. Oh, who was she kidding? It wasn't unexpected. She already missed Carson and that spelled trouble with a capital T.

CHAPTER THREE

Sienna pulled into her driveway, exhausted from the day she'd had. And completely wired at the same time, all because she'd seen Carson.

Twice.

Sighing at herself, she headed inside but as soon as she stepped into her mudroom, she froze. Normally her security system chirped, the loud beeps a signal that she needed to disable it within forty-five seconds. Now there was simply the little *beep beep* of her door opening.

But nothing else.

And she was absolutely neurotic about setting her alarm every day because of what she did for a living.

For the most part the clients she dealt with were angry at someone, whether it be a spouse or whoever, but at the end of the day she was just a PI. A small weapon in whatever war they were waging against each other. Still, there were a few occasions where people had been stupid and vengeful, so she was cautious.

Easing back out the door, she hurried to her car. Instinct buzzing through her like angry mosquitos, she opened the garage door and hurriedly reversed into her driveway.

She was probably being stupid but there was always that one percent chance that— Her heart stopped for a millisecond as a masked man wearing dark gloves stepped into her garage. The door was closing on him as he took a step in her direction.

Holy sweet potatoes!

Heart racing, she pressed on the gas, flooring it into reverse.

In hindsight, she hadn't even looked back to see if anyone was in the street, her eyes glued to the man standing there.

She quickly kicked it into drive, racing down the road even as she yanked her cell phone out.

Without questioning why, she called Carson instead of 911. Sure he was the police, but she'd still called him and was surprised when he picked up on the second ring.

"Hey gorgeous," he murmured, his voice sex and sin.

She had another jolt of a different kind upon hearing him call her gorgeous, but she quickly moved past that. "Someone broke into my house. A masked man."

"Don't go inside," he ordered.

"I'm in my car, driving away," she rushed out, wild horses still galloping in her chest as she checked her rearview mirror. Everything felt so surreal right now. She knew what she'd seen and it *still* didn't feel real. Her fingers tightly gripped the steering wheel, her knuckles pale as she came up to a stop sign. She glanced all around her, fear ratcheting up inside her.

She realized she was heading straight toward Carson's place, which was also ridiculous. Or maybe not. Her instinct was telling her to get somewhere safe. No matter their personal history, in a situation like this he would keep her safe.

She glanced in the rearview mirror. No one was following her. The horses in her chest eased up a bit, but not by much.

"Get somewhere safe. I'm calling in the nearest patrol right now," he said before there was a muffled sound and she heard another voice. He was talking to someone and she wondered if he was still at whatever had called him away before. A crime scene, she'd assumed. He came back on the line again. "Where are you now?"

She quickly gave him her location as she kept driving, trying to put distance between herself and her house.

"Okay, get to the Publix about two blocks from where you are. Go sit in a brightly lit section of the parking lot. I'm three minutes out."

"Will do." She was glad that her voice didn't shake, though she had no idea how it wasn't at this point. A tremble had started in her core and she couldn't seem to stop it as she took a left-hand turn.

Someone had been *in* her house, her sanctuary. They'd broken in and done God only knew what inside. That someone had been waiting, could have attacked her if she'd ignored her instinct and gone inside.

A wave of nausea swelled up suddenly, but she managed to shove it back down. She hadn't gone inside and she was safe.

For now.

"Talk to me, Sienna. I need to hear your voice." Carson's tone was soft, soothing as he talked to her, and she realized she'd just gone silent as she got caught up in her thoughts.

She cleared her throat. "I'm here, I'm fine. I just..." She cleared her throat again as the words stuck. "Thank you for answering," she rasped out, so damn grateful that he'd picked up, that he was coming to see her.

That he'd be involved with whatever this was. Because even if she didn't want a relationship with him, she trusted Carson to help her.

"I'll always answer for you."

It didn't take her long to get to the Publix, and even though she was still terrified, panic buzzing through her like angry bees, she found a spot near the front, thankfully. So she sat in her locked Jeep and waited.

* * *

Carson put his hand at the small of Sienna's back as they stepped into her house—and ignored the look his partner gave him. Because Julian Ruiz missed nothing and it was clear Sienna mattered to Carson.

Plus, he'd had too many drinks one night months ago and told Julian about her.

"As far as we can see, nothing has been overly disturbed and we've got a small team searching for hidden cameras and microphones in case this has to do with your job," he said quietly as they moved through to her kitchen.

Sienna nodded at him then glanced at Julian, but didn't say anything else. Her expression had a pinched quality and he hated that this had happened to her.

No matter what, he was going to get to the bottom of it. Because a masked man breaking into her place? There could be multiple reasons for that, none of them good.

"I just don't understand how he got in here," she murmured to herself as she opened two cabinet doors and rummaged inside.

"We found a few scratches on the lock on your back door. And your alarm was obviously off."

"No, I set it. I *always* set it." She headed out of the kitchen and straight for the living room.

"Maybe you forgot." He stayed with her, but gave her enough space to search for anything that might be missing.

She started walking around, methodically looking at everything, opening the doors to an entertainment center. The flat-screen on the wall was still in place and other electronics scattered around the room appeared to have been untouched as well. Julian had dusted for prints in a few places, but Sienna had said the guy was wearing gloves—and Carson trusted her recollection and observation skills.

"No," she finally said, referring to his statement minutes earlier. "I'm so neurotic about programing my security system. I mean, I guess there's a one percent chance I forgot to set it on the same day someone broke in—" She let out a low curse, then pulled her phone out of her back pocket.

"What is it?"

"I can't believe I didn't think of this before," she muttered to herself. "I can just check my dashboard and check the log."

He moved up next to her, ignoring her fresh vanilla scent as he looked down at her screen.

"Someone turned my alarm off in the house an hour before I got home. Manually, according to this." Her cheeks had gone white as she handed him her phone so he could see the activity log.

It was similar to the one he had, breaking down when the security panels were disarmed, armed, even when her doors opened and closed.

So this was definitely not a random break-in. Because breaking a security system took a decent amount of skill. Unless... "Does anyone know your code? Have you ever texted it to someone, given it to your mom or...anyone?"

Sienna paused, her dark green eyes thoughtful as she looked at him. "I don't think so, but I can't swear to it. I change my code every two months or so and I recently changed it. Since then I haven't given it to anyone. Though I have given my mom the code in the past when I've been out of town. She's the only one though."

"What about your brothers? Maybe you texted them?"

"No way. I love them, but..." She shook her head as she trailed off.

"Hmm." Her security panel was in her laundry room on the wall right by the door so the panel wasn't visible from any windows, which eliminated the possibility of someone spying on her that way. "Do you think this has anything to do with one of your cases? A recent one or a current one?" Maybe something to do with the yacht she'd broken into today.

"It's definitely possible. But…I don't know the purpose of breaking in here. Most of my stuff is at my office and I back everything up to the cloud anyway. So hurting me won't change the outcome of anything else. So…I need to think," she said, more to herself than him as she strode out of the living room.

He followed her, his gaze trailing down her back, over her perfect ass, and her long jean-clad legs. She moved with an innate confidence that was the sexiest thing about her.

Her dark brown hair was still pulled back into that braid against her head and she moved with purpose, every sleek line of her making him itch to touch, to stroke and kiss.

Even though he was keeping himself locked down now, it was impossible not to want her, not when he'd kissed every inch of her. It was more than physical though. He'd made it clear he wanted to date her. Hell, he'd had to hold back because he hadn't wanted to scare her, but after three dates she'd told him they would just be friends and had stopped texting or calling him. He was ninety percent sure it wasn't anything he'd done either.

The chemistry between them had been combustible—still was.

"My old laptop is missing," she said as she shut the closet door of a bedroom she'd turned into a home office. Then she went over to a cabinet and opened it. "So is one of my old cameras. Damn it, my long-range camera is gone too."

There was no computer on her desk and she'd left her laptop bag in his truck—which was currently locked. "You just have the laptop?"

"A laptop, a tablet, a newer camera, my phone. And my phone and laptop are synced."

"What about paper files?" He didn't see any filing cabinets, but wanted to cover all his bases. Even if he wasn't officially going to be running this case.

"I don't keep anything like that here. But I use my office when I'm working on a case, getting things organized for my clients. I like having this personal space in case I don't want to go into the office."

He nodded, glanced around the small room. It had her stamp all over it. Eclectic art, colorful, gauzy, billowing curtains over the window, a little ceramic hedgehog with a top hat as her pen holder.

"You can't stay here tonight," he said as she continued to look around the room, opening more drawers and shutting them.

"I know," she said absently. "I'm going to call Daniel, see if I can stay with him and Kathryn."

"Just stay with me." The words were out before he could think about them, but Carson stood by them.

She straightened at that, her whole body going rigid as she turned to face him. Her eyes narrowed ever so slightly as she watched him carefully. "Seriously?"

"Look, we don't know who broke into your house. And I don't like the fact that he was masked, or the fact that he disarmed your security system. This isn't some amateur hack job. He took very specific things and it stands to reason that he hasn't got what he wants yet—so he's not done. He'll want your current laptop once he realizes what he has is useless." At least that was what Carson was guessing based on past cases and common sense. "If he decides to come after you, do you want to lead him back to your family?"

Now she full-on glared at him—and he still wanted to kiss her, wanted to smooth away the frown lines. "Well, if you're going to get all logical on me," she muttered. "I can stay in the guest room." She paused, her expression softening as she seemed to lose all her steam. "And thank you. I appreciate it." She ran a hand down her braid as she looked around her office again, sighing. "I hate that someone was in my space. It makes me feel violated."

"We'll catch whoever did this. And you're going to need to make an official statement to my partner."

She looked back at him, her braid swishing slightly with the movement. "Not to you?"

"It's unlikely I'll be directly on this case. Not with our relationship." He held up a hand when she started to say something. "You're my sister's sister-in-law, and that constitutes a relationship. But Julian will keep me in the loop. Plus…I'll also be working on it, just not officially."

She looked as if she wanted to say more, but nodded. "Can I grab some clothes and toiletries?"

"Get whatever you want. Julian will put someone on your house for now, not that I think anyone is coming back after this. At least not anytime soon."

Expression tight, she simply nodded and headed out of the office for her bedroom.

Instead of following after her, he went to find his partner and update him on what she'd found.

Whoever had decided to mess with Sienna had taken on Carson without knowing it. Because no one was going to mess with her and get away with it.

CHAPTER FOUR

Carson's gaze fell on Sienna the moment she entered the kitchen. Like that proverbial moth to a flame, if she was anywhere in the vicinity, his eyes were on her. She was like a magnet for him. A tall, sexy, smart-mouthed magnet he couldn't get enough of. "How are you feeling?"

"My brain is a little fried." She sighed and sat at his kitchen table, crossing one lean leg over the other. She was wearing little shorts and a tank top and her hair was damp against her head. It was the second time that day she'd showered at his place, though this time he thought was more to calm her down than anything else. "Are you sure you don't mind me staying here?" Her foot tapped nervously as she watched him.

"Why would I mind?"

She lifted a shoulder, the action jerky. "I don't want to put you in danger."

He snorted in response and went to the stovetop where he pulled the teapot off the burner and poured a mug of hot water for her.

She inhaled slightly as he set it in front of her. "I didn't know you drank tea," she murmured.

"I don't. I remembered you said you liked chamomile tea at night." So he'd bought some in case she ever decided to stay over. But then when he'd pushed for just a little bit more from her, relationship-wise, she'd iced him out completely. It still stung.

"Oh..." She cleared her throat. "Ah, thank you." Then she avoided his gaze and took a sip of her tea, sighing as she set it back on the tabletop. "So when do you think I'll be able to go back to my house?"

"Do you really want to go back right now?" he asked dryly.

"No." She let out a little shudder and wrapped her arms around herself. In that moment, he wished he had the right to comfort her. "I just meant like, when do you think it will be safe?"

Sighing, he sat at the table across from her. He wished he had an answer, hated that she was displaced and scared and everything was up in the air. "There are too many unknowns right now. And I don't like the thought of you going back to a place where someone hacked your security so easily."

She tapped her finger against her mug, her expression thoughtful. "I started making a list of recent cases, the ones I wrapped up."

"What about the one you're working on now?"

"I'm including that one too. But I can't imagine why my client's husband would come after me. He probably doesn't even know that I discovered his yacht and other assets yet. Or he could have—because she might have already called her lawyer."

"Hiding a yacht," Carson muttered.

She snorted in agreement. "Right? It's so obnoxious. So..." She cleared her throat, her smile dimming. "I'll get my file together and send it to you or your partner?"

"Just make it both of us." Because he'd be working this case too even if he wasn't officially on it. Nothing could stop him from finding out who'd tried to hurt Sienna.

* * *

Sitting on the guest bed in Carson's condo, Sienna impatiently tapped her finger against her mug of tea as the phone rang once, twice...

"Hey, I was just talking about you." Eileen's voice was bright and cheerful even with the later hour.

"I hope you were saying only good things."

Her client laughed. "Oh, definitely. My soon-to-be ex is almost sure to settle now. I contacted Valentina with all the information you gave me and she's reached out to his attorney."

"Already?"

"Yep. I wasn't going to sit on this. I want this wrapped up and done with. And I'm sure he does too, even if he doesn't want to settle with me."

Well, that answered Sienna's question about whether Eileen had already contacted Valentina, the attorney who often recommended Sienna's services. She'd reached out to her because she wanted to talk to all her current clients in case the break-in at her place had anything to do with anyone she'd worked for.

"I just wish I could have seen his face when he saw those pictures you took!" She let out a laugh that was just a little too loud and Sienna wondered if she'd been drinking. "It feels a bit petty but I love that he's getting this information on a Friday night. I hope it ruins his whole weekend. Bastard."

"I'm glad things are moving forward for you."

"Thanks. Hey, is everything okay?"

"Oh yeah, fine. I'd only called to see if you'd contacted Valentina about everything. I called her but she didn't answer."

"Probably because she's talking to the slime's attorney right now." Another laugh-snort of glee.

"Listen..." Sienna tried to find the right words, wanted to say this carefully. "Someone broke into my house earlier."

"Oh my God, are you okay?"

"I'm fine. The police are handling it but...I don't know if it had anything to do with any of my cases. I just wanted to let you know so you could stay safe and just take extra precautions." Sienna wouldn't be able to live with herself if she didn't say something and then Eileen got hurt.

"Thanks for the heads-up. I'm actually in Miami already. A friend of mine flew us down on her private plane and I'm staying here for a bit."

"I'm glad to hear that." She'd certainly sleep better knowing that Eileen was out of the city.

Once they wrapped things up Sienna tried Valentina again, but got no answer. After texting her, she pulled up her files and started compiling a list even as sleep pushed in on her. This bed was so comfy and inviting and her brain was more than done for the day.

She was so tempted to shut her laptop and search Carson out—maybe see if he wanted her to join him in his bed. But nope. She had more self-control than that.

Hopefully.

CHAPTER FIVE

The next morning Sienna stumbled into Carson's kitchen, the scent of rich coffee filling the air. Normally she was a morning person, but she was dragging today. After tossing and turning for ages, she'd finally snagged a few hours of rest, but it hadn't been solid sleep and she was feeling it now.

For some reason she wasn't surprised that sexy-as-sin Carson was already at his kitchen table, working away on his laptop. The man looked wide-awake with damp hair, a T-shirt that molded to annoyingly muscular biceps, and a cup of coffee steaming in front of him.

"Did you get any sleep last night?" she murmured as she headed straight for the coffeepot.

"A little bit." He glanced over at her, his gaze lingering on her bare legs for a long moment.

A shiver of delight rolled through her, waking her up as much as she imagined her first shot of caffeine would. He should *not* be able to affect her with just one look, but there it was. The man was her weakness.

"Your guest bed is soft." She poured herself a mug, inhaled the pure goodness.

"*My* bed is more comfortable." His tone was dry, pulling a startled laugh from her.

"It's too early for that kind of talk," she murmured as she turned to face him. No way were they going to talk about "them" or...whatever. No relationship talk. Because they didn't have one other than friendship. That was all. Still...his bed was soft, dang it.

"Or maybe it's exactly the right time. Maybe I can get you to finally tell me why you threw up all those walls between us after we had sex." Carson shifted in his chair, stretched out his long, muscular legs that even jeans couldn't hide. His dark hair was slightly mussed and he still hadn't shaved so his scruff was a bit longer and oh God, it looked good on him. His tattoos peeked out from his T-shirt and she had to resist the urge to look at them—to walk right up to him and take his face in her hands. To kiss him the way her entire body craved.

She could feel the full weight of his attention on her and, pre-caffeine, that was a whole lot. Clearly she wasn't thinking because she was so tempted to just throw caution to the wind and jump this man. And something told her that he'd let her. Heck, he'd welcome it. Oh no. No, no, no.

Drink your coffee, girl!

Sienna turned away from him, unable to handle that intense stare as she hurried to the fridge to grab some creamer. "Look," she said on a sigh. "You don't want *me*. You just like the *idea* of me." And it was better that they got that out of the way now.

He snorted with laughter as she turned to face him. Damn it, it was like he got sexier every single time she looked at him. "Please tell me more about this insane idea that you have."

She wrapped her fingers around the mug, frowned at him over the rim. "It's not crazy, and I'm right. You don't want me."

He laughed again, shaking his head now, as if she'd lost her mind.

"Look, I have a fairly dangerous job," she said.

"I know. So do I." He lifted a shoulder as if to say *So what?*

But she knew better. "You want someone softer, someone who works a regular nine-to-five and who doesn't get put into dangerous situations."

He simply lifted an eyebrow as he watched her. "Where the hell are you getting this from?"

"You wouldn't be the first guy who couldn't handle my job." Wouldn't be the first guy in law enforcement either. She'd tried dating someone in law enforcement before. A DEA agent, not a detective, but he definitely hadn't been able to handle her job. Not only that, but he'd tried to tell her what to do, as if she'd asked for his help.

And if things went south with her and Carson, it would be so complicated because of their families. It wasn't like they could avoid each other forever. Nope, they'd be stuck having awkward conversations every time they saw each other and just, no, no, no.

He frowned at her. "For the record, I like what you do. I think your job is interesting. I think *you* are interesting. I've never said I want you to change your job. I'm not sure where this crap is coming from, but it's not from me."

"Crap?"

"Yeah. I like that you go toe-to-toe with me. I like that you're a smart-ass. I like a *lot* about you. Even when you're driving me crazy," he said as he turned back to his laptop. Then he started muttering under his breath to something on the screen. Before she could think about responding, he said, "Tell me about Kevin Fox."

She paused before she took another sip of her coffee. It went down smooth and hot, but she focused on the man Carson had just brought up on his screen. "Fox is a loser. But he's in jail."

"What happened with that case?" he prodded.

She'd included Fox's name in her list of recent cases for Carson, but hadn't given much detail because, well, Fox was in jail.

"Not much to tell. He used to knock his wife, Hailey, around until she finally got up the courage to leave him once she was pregnant. He lost his mind when she tried to leave. He already hurt her badly, on a fairly continual basis. But he was smart about the way he abused her, leaving no marks that anyone could see, and she would never press charges."

"The guy's brother is a cop?" He looked at his screen, his expression going darker.

"Yeah. But that guy is all right from what I can tell. He had no idea what his brother was doing, but Fox made it sound like she would have no one to turn to, that no one would believe her. And she believed him. It was like he brainwashed her into thinking she was trash." Sienna wished she could punch the guy again just for good measure.

"How did you get introduced to the wife?"

"A friend of mine, an attorney, took her case pro bono. And she recommended that Hailey hire me—I also worked for her pro bono, although she made me a quilt as a thank-you."

Carson half-smiled at that.

"Anyway, I followed him for a while, got some really interesting pictures of him committing random crimes. He was just a piece of shit in general and he likely would've gotten himself tossed in jail sooner or later. He'd already been arrested and jailed a couple times, but I took what I had and turned it over to the police. Somehow he found out it was me, and when he was out on bail he stopped by my office talking trash, trying to intimidate me. He also had a weapon on him, though he didn't use it. When I refused to back down, I could see the shock on his face. He eventually took a swing at me but he missed and I broke his nose. He tried to say that I attacked him, but unfortunately for him I've got security cameras in my office for that very reason."

He lifted an eyebrow. "Damn."

"You think he might be involved?" Maybe the guy's brother had wanted revenge or something? But no, Sienna found that hard to believe. Fox's brother had seemed pretty decent, had been getting Hailey stuff for the baby, doing a lot of work around the house for her. And the break-in at Sienna's place had been too methodical, too clean. Someone had been looking for something specific and Fox was nothing more than a blunt object with no finesse. The guy was in jail anyway.

"I don't know anything at this point, but you didn't have much next to his name other than the words 'asshole' and 'deserves another broken nose,' so I wanted to ask." Amusement flared in his blue eyes and she fought the effect that had on her.

She was already on a slippery slope with Carson. Because everything he did affected her. "Sorry about that," she murmured, wincing. "I was exhausted last night. Let me look back over what I sent you." She'd tossed together a file for Carson and his partner, wanting to give them as much information as possible, but clearly she'd been half asleep while putting it together.

"Tell me about this guy, Leo Tizon. You don't have much next to his name either."

She drank more coffee, savored it. "There's not much next to him because he's a new client. He hired me because he thinks his partner is screwing him out of money. They own a bunch of food trucks and the margin of profit is already fairly slim. But he thinks his partner is siphoning money away a little at a time."

"Is he?"

She lifted a shoulder. "I'm not sure yet. But I'm pretty sure his partner is screwing his wife. So, not exactly a stand-up person."

Carson winced. "You really see people at their worst, don't you," he murmured.

She wasn't surprised by his insight. His job was different than hers, but he still saw people at their worst too. "No more than you, I imagine."

He paused and then nodded. "Yeah. I usually see people on their worst day. Or at least on a really bad one. Sometimes I have to remind myself of that when they're acting like assholes. Trauma can bring out the worst in people and they react poorly."

"Do you like what you do?" She'd never asked him before and she was curious.

He nodded and turned in his chair, once again giving her the full weight of that blue stare.

It was a little bit intimidating to be on the receiving end of all that sexiness.

"I do," he said. "I like solving puzzles. Kinda like you. And I like helping people get justice." He paused, a heavy weight hanging in the air as if he wanted to say more.

"What?"

"When I was in college, I was friends with a girl who was raped. The detective handling her case was, well, lazy. A piece of shit if I'm going to be blunt. He didn't handle the case the way he should have, treated her more like a suspect than a victim. She never got the justice she deserved and it always stuck with me. I'm not saying it's the only reason I became a detective, but it's part of it. That whole thing stuck with me. Our system is broken in a whole lot of ways and I want to be part of the solution."

She took another sip of her coffee, not surprised by his view of the world. He had a sort of code of honor she'd seen early on. It was impossible not to respect that. "How's your friend? Did she recover, emotionally?"

He smiled slightly, an affection bleeding into his gaze. "She's really good. Really happy now with her new husband. The man treats her like gold. And the guy…" He cleared his throat, a hint of anger flashing in his eyes. "The man who hurt her ended up going to jail for a similar crime. I'm not happy about what he did, but I'm glad he got caught and someone did their job for once."

"The world is screwed up," she murmured.

"No kidding." He cleared his throat. "Okay, so this new case with the two partners. Can you think of any reason the partner would come after you? Has he seen you following him?"

"No. And trust me on that. He's not very bright." She'd gotten pictures of him and his client's wife at a cheap motel. It was like something out of a bad movie. They weren't very clever about their meeting places and didn't hide their PDA even in public. They were like octopuses all over each other. Almost like they wanted to get caught.

"What about the yacht case, the one with the Bentleys?"

"I really can't think of anything new from my files. She's definitely going to get a bigger settlement, but the guy can afford it. I've looked into his financials and he is killing it. What she wants won't even put a dent in his lifestyle or income. Not really. And she already has the pictures. So does her attorney. So why come after me? What's the point?" Sienna figured the guy could have just come after her because he was a jerk, but that seemed like a waste of time.

Carson looked back at his computer and typed in some more notes. "I'm going to update Julian with everything you've told me."

"What's he working on today? Can you tell me?"

"He's following up with some of your former clients. Well, not clients, but the people your actual clients hired you to look into."

She'd figured as much. While she really didn't like talking about her clients with anyone, they all knew that if she was ever involved in a police investigation she would cooperate with the cops. That and a few other things she'd made clear up front. And all of her clients had signed off on their contracts.

"You hungry?" Carson asked suddenly. "I think I've got bacon in the fridge."

"Coffee is fine."

He eyed her. "Are you just saying that because you don't want me to cook?"

"I don't want you to go to any trouble." He was already putting her up at his place.

"Fine, then *I'm* hungry, so I'm going to make some bacon and eggs. How does that sound?"

She grinned at him. "Delicious. And if you're taking requests, I really like scrambled eggs with salsa."

He grinned at her and it softened his entire face, making all sorts of heat pool low in her belly. "I'll make whatever you want." His voice dropped an octave as he said it.

And she knew she was in trouble. This man was so dangerous to her. Wild, hot danger in the sexiest package ever.

She cleared her throat and pushed away from the countertop. "Thanks. I'm going to get changed and organize my notes a little bit better. Plus I need to check in with my current client. I know I'm sort of in lockdown right now, but I still need to work."

"Of course. Breakfast won't take too long."

She made her escape, wondering if holing up with Carson had been the best idea. Because she knew that if she asked either of her brothers, or heck, her parents, they'd let her stay with them and she'd be safe. But then she'd be caged, basically, and unable to contribute to this investigation.

She simply couldn't sit on the sidelines. And...she really liked staying under the same roof as Carson, no matter how badly she wanted to deny it.

CHAPTER SIX

Feeling more awake after getting dressed for the day and updating that file, Sienna stepped into the kitchen to find Carson eating and a plate of bacon and scrambled eggs across the table from him. "Oh my gosh, you're the best. Thank you so much for cooking. I could—" She cleared her throat as she sat, definitely not about to finish *that* thought.

"You could what?"

"I could probably eat a whole pound of bacon," she said, lying through her teeth. She'd been about to say that she could get used to this—as in, she could get used to being with him. Which was true and terrifying, so she wasn't opening up that Pandora's box. "Anything new since I saw you half an hour ago?"

He shook his head, watching her carefully. Damn that man and his detective skills. His scrutiny made her feel exposed, as if he could see right through to her innermost thoughts.

She ignored him and bit into a piece of crispy bacon, moaning slightly. It was even cooked the way she loved it. As they ate in silence, him working on his laptop as she checked through work emails, she noticed how comforting it was to be with him. Just his mere presence made her feel safe and secure.

She frowned as a text popped up from Daniel. Then one from Brodie. She winced as she read both messages from her brothers. Then one from Kathryn popped up.

Carson told us what happened. What do you need? I've got a place you can stay no problem. This one from Daniel.

I can pick you up right now. What do you need, little sis? From Brodie.

Omg! Are you okay? Carson told me what happened. Do you want to come stay with us? I've got a room and bottle of wine ready for you! From Kathryn.

"You told my brothers what happened?" She set her phone down, deciding to ignore all their messages and her phone for a moment.

"Of course." He said it as if she should have expected it. "Told Kathryn too." And he looked completely unapologetic.

She bristled slightly. "You couldn't let me tell them?"

He lifted a shoulder, a very broad, sexy one she wanted to trail her fingers over. "Daniel's married to my sister. If someone decides to target your family to get to you, I wanted to give them a heads-up. It would have been irresponsible of me not to say anything."

"You're annoying when you're right." She bit into another piece of bacon, the crunch satisfying.

"Unfortunately for you I'm right all the time."

"Keep telling yourself that." She ate another piece of bacon, tried not to moan too loudly.

He simply grinned at her before he polished off the rest of his eggs.

She'd started to ask what his agenda was for the day when his phone dinged quietly.

She knew something was wrong even though his expression barely changed as he looked at the screen. It was something about the way he went *very* still as he read whatever it was.

"What is it?" She was nosy, and if it involved the break-in at her place, she wanted to know.

"The attorney you work with sometimes, the one who recommends clients call you..." His expression was sober, his jaw going tight.

"I work with a few attorneys. Which one are you talking about?"

"Valentina Hall."

The breakfast she'd just eaten turned to stone in her stomach. Sienna cleared her throat, forced the question out even though she didn't want the answer. "What about her?"

He paused for a long moment. "She was found murdered, and her office torched."

The words were a sucker punch to her sternum. Her instinct was to ask him if he was sure, but of course he was. "When?" she rasped out.

"Yesterday, mid-evening. She called her husband, told him she'd be working late and then when she didn't come home... Well, you can figure out the rest. Julian just let me know. He doesn't like that you're linked to her and just had a break-in, and she was..." Carson shook his head slightly. "I'm sorry."

Even though she hadn't finished her breakfast, Sienna pushed the plate away. "She has kids," she murmured. It was awful regardless, but Sienna still hated the thought of those kids growing up without their mom.

Carson nodded slightly, as if he already knew.

"I'll go over every single client she's recommended and give you a comprehensive list."

It could be a coincidence that Sienna's house had been broken into by a masked intruder the same day Valentina had been killed, but she was going to go with the odds on this one. The two things were related.

She rubbed her hands over her face, trying to wrap her mind around this. "I know it's soon, but do they have any suspects? You know there's security cameras at her place and across the street, and—"

"Julian's on top of this. I promise." Carson's expression was sympathetic.

"Can I call her husband?"

"I'd wait a little bit. Julian just left the husband and he'll likely be telling their kids soon."

Fighting the nausea pushing up, Sienna stood, picking up her plate and his, taking them to the sink. Wanting to keep her hands busy, she washed the dishes as she started mentally reviewing all the clients Valentina had ever sent her. She couldn't believe that Valentina was dead, hated that her family would be grieving and dealing with the aftermath of senseless violence.

If this involved one of her cases and Sienna could help in any way, she sure as hell was going to. Because she wouldn't sit idly by and do nothing.

* * *

After taking a few moments to splash water on her face and get herself together, Sienna stepped back into the kitchen to find Carson on his cell phone.

He nodded once at her, his expression hard as he spoke to someone.

She set up her laptop across from his, figuring this was going to be their workstation for the time being. She knew she should probably call her brothers but didn't feel like dealing with either of them right now. She loved them more than anything but they could be a whole lot of overprotectiveness. She texted them, and Kathryn, however, just to let them know she was safe.

"You're sure?" Carson said. "All right. Keep me informed." He ended his phone call and his expression didn't change as she looked at him. "Fox is out of jail."

Ice wrapped around her. "Are you serious?"

"Yep. Got out a few days ago. Overcrowding and some other bullshit reasons, but he's out."

Sienna stood, though she wasn't sure what the hell she planned to do. "Oh God, Hailey. His ex-wife."

"She's out of town apparently. Julian has already looked into it. She's visiting family in Canada and is out of the country for the next couple weeks."

Sienna let out a sigh, the tension in her chest unraveling slightly. "At least there's that. Has Julian brought him in for questioning yet?"

"Nope. He doesn't have a parole officer or anything to check in with, and no credit cards or cell phone that we know of, so finding him is going to be a task."

"We'll just see about that," she said as she pulled up her file on Fox. She'd made a list of all of his contacts and people he'd screwed over. She was going to find where the loser was hiding out. And if he was behind killing Valentina, she was going to make sure he went to jail for life.

CHAPTER SEVEN

Carson tucked his cell phone into his back pocket as he stepped into the kitchen. He'd been making phone calls all day, helping Julian as much as possible from here. Normally they worked as a team on all of their investigations and divided up interrogations and research, but his number one priority was keeping eyes on Sienna. On keeping her safe.

He had a feeling that would always be his priority.

"I found him!" Sienna did a fist pump as she looked up from her laptop, her wide grin triumphant.

He had to shake himself out of staring at her. "Found who?"

"Fox."

He shouldn't be surprised, but a thread of it wound its way through him. "Seriously? How?"

She lifted an eyebrow as she closed her laptop and stood, stretching. As she arched her back he had to force himself not to stare at the way her breasts pulled against her T-shirt. She was tall, lean, built like a runner. And he'd seen her in action before—she could outrun him any day of the week. He knew she'd participated in multiple marathons. Which didn't surprise him, knowing her personality. She was driven and couldn't seem to sit still. She'd told him that she'd been diagnosed late in high school with ADHD and the diagnosis had changed everything for her. She'd embraced that part of herself and learned how to make her ADHD work for her instead of against her.

"I probably don't want to know how you found him, right." He didn't phrase it as a question.

"I didn't do anything illegal." She tried to look offended but she ended up grinning again, looking pleased with herself. "I simply called a few people who I know had a beef with him before he went to prison. People he stole from. Turns out he's crashing at the house of someone he used to smoke weed with. The guy is in the Bahamas for the week and said Fox could lie low at his place while he got back on his feet."

"You have the address?"

She groaned. "You're going to give this to your partner, aren't you?"

"Yes."

"I was hoping we could—"

"You're not going anywhere."

She rolled her eyes but rattled off the address to him anyway, and crossed her arms over her chest. "I need to get out of here for at least ten minutes. Can we go to the gym or something?"

Shaking his head, he texted Julian before looking back up at her. "We can go to the gym here or there's a track that loops around a park close by. I know you like to run."

Her eyes lit up and he stupidly felt like a king. "You think we'll be okay doing that?"

"No one knows you're here and we won't be going anyplace with cameras..." He frowned as he looked back down at his pinging phone. "Julian is stuck in interviews right now and doesn't want to chance that Fox slips away."

"Do we need to bring him in?"

"There is no we." They could send an officer over to talk to Fox, but they had no reason to truly bring him in. And Fox understood the system, would know that. Carson needed to talk to him in person, wanted to see his expression when he told him that Valentina Hall had been murdered.

"So you're going to leave me here by myself?" Her tone and body language were challenging.

"Fine. If you come with me, you will stay in the truck the whole time. I'm just going to talk to him and ask him to come in to answer some questions. Got it?"

Her smile was way too big and way too sexy as she nodded enthusiastically. "I'll wear a hat and sunglasses on the drive over."

* * *

Carson glanced around the quiet neighborhood. This was an older Florida neighborhood, the kind that had mostly retirees. Almost all ranch-style houses, jalousie windows and ADT stickers on street-facing windows even though most of them likely didn't have security systems installed.

"What did we talk about?" he asked as he put his truck in park.

"Oh my God, you're ridiculous." Sienna was practically bouncing in her seat, this never-ending fountain of energy. She'd pulled her hair up into a ponytail and it swished every time she moved. Which was a lot. "I'm not getting out. Promise."

He'd already run the license plate of the sedan under the carport and it had come back as registered to the owner of the house. The guy Sienna said was in the Bahamas. "Okay. I just wanted to make sure there was no miscommunication between us. You shouldn't even be with me, but since you've consulted with the PD before, it should be all right." She shouldn't be with him at all, especially not on an active investigation, but as of now Fox wasn't technically linked to this case. He might be once Carson questioned him, but that was up in the air.

"Just go knock on the door. Get him to come into the station. Use that charm of yours," she added.

He couldn't tell if she was being sarcastic or not and resisted the urge to lean over and brush his lips over hers. He certainly didn't have that right but the urge to kiss her was there nonetheless. Always there, lingering.

He couldn't get her out of his mind, not when she'd so thoroughly burrowed herself under his skin. This woman was in his blood at this point. And he was questioning his own sanity for continuing to want her so damn badly.

Sunglasses on, he slid out of the truck and scanned the neighborhood. He waved once at the older woman watering the yard across the street.

The woman was wearing a housedress, her gray hair curled perfectly. Didn't wave back, just watched him cautiously.

According to the computer run he had done, the owner of this house had inherited it when his mom died. And if the guy was into drugs as Fox was, it stood to reason that the neighbors didn't care for the owner or any associates.

After another quick scan of the street, he hurried up to the front door, knocked once. As he did, he realized the door was already ajar.

Nudging it open with his boot, he called out. "Kevin Fox? My name's Carson Irish. I'm with the police."

The door creaked as it swung open, and that was when he spotted what was most definitely blood pooling in the hallway from an open doorway. *Shit.*

Moving quickly, he withdrew his weapon and swept inside. As he moved, he called in backup before sweeping the rest of the house. He went room by room, methodically checking each room, but when he was done there was only one dead body sprawled on the tile of the small bathroom.

Kevin Fox with a bullet hole right through his head.

CHAPTER EIGHT

Carson looked out the window from his boss's office to the bullpen where Sienna was sitting at his desk. She was talking on her phone, likely to one of her brothers, as they'd been calling her all day.

He quickly reverted his attention back to his boss, Captain Tobias Johnson.

"I think we need to get Sienna out of town," Carson said bluntly, looking between his boss and partner. Someone had broken into her house, stolen electronics, an attorney she'd worked for was dead, and someone she'd investigated was dead. She did not need to be anywhere near here right now.

Julian simply nodded because ultimately it was the captain's decision, not theirs.

Tobias was quiet for a long moment. At six feet with broad shoulders that highlighted his high school linebacker days, his boss had a commanding presence. "I don't like any of this, especially the optics if this gets out."

Carson knew what he meant even though his boss didn't say it out loud. Sienna was a MacArthur, and one of her brothers owned a large company and had been voted sexiest bachelor a bunch of years in a row. The other owned his own security firm and worked for one of the biggest tech companies on the East Coast. Not to mention her wealthy parents were well-known in the region for all their charitable work.

"She won't stay with her family," Carson said. "But she's agreed to go out of town with me. One of her brothers has access to a place in Miami where we can lie low." It wasn't true that she'd agreed, but he would convince her. Because after this recent murder, he simply wanted Sienna away from here. Yes, he wanted to investigate, but he trusted Julian, and sometimes it was wise to know when to step back. Right now his job was to keep her safe. Period. Because if she stayed here, she was going to be a bigger target.

And she might not like it, but in the end she would see that he was right. He just had to convince her to leave with him.

"I trust your judgment," his boss finally said. "We need to make sure we keep her potential involvement with the two murders quiet as long as possible. We need her safe. Do what you've got to do. I want all the details later, but get her out of town."

Carson was surprised at how quickly his boss was moving on this but maybe he shouldn't be. Tobias had always been a big-picture type of boss and had never micromanaged.

His boss continued, his expression darkening. "And I want answers," he snapped out. "Two people are dead. I don't want any more deaths."

"We're working around the clock." Julian's tone was neutral.

Carson simply stood and nodded because it didn't matter what they said at this point.

"She really agreed to go with you?" Julian asked once they were out in the bullpen, the door shut behind them.

He snorted softly.

His partner cracked a smile, the first one Carson had seen in a while. "Why do I get the feeling that you're going to have a hard time convincing her?"

"Shut it," he muttered as he reached his desk.

Sienna popped up immediately. "Is everything okay? What did your boss say?"

"Everything's good." Good being a relative word. But she was alive, and he was going to make sure she stayed that way.

"You're not in trouble?" she asked.

He blinked. "No. That's not why we were in there."

She eyed him carefully as if she wasn't sure she believed him. "All right. So what's our next move?"

"To get you somewhere safe. I've already talked to Daniel, and—"

"I'm not staying with my family. My parents are out of town and my brothers will smother me. Not to mention, I—"

"Can I finish?" he asked.

She bit her bottom lip, looking ridiculously sexy. "Sorry."

"As I was saying." He lowered his voice. "I want to get out of town with you. Just the two of us so you can lie low. If someone is gunning for you, they won't find you here."

"Where are you thinking of going?"

"Miami. Daniel said a friend of his owns a condo there you can stay at. It's not being rented right now so there will be no connection to your family."

"Miami? Okay."

He paused, suspicious. "You gave in really quickly."

"You were expecting an argument?"

"Yes."

"Look, I want to be smart. And I've already talked to a friend of mine. He's going to take over the case with Leo Tizon. Leo is fine with it."

Even if he hadn't been, Carson was getting her out of here. Still, she had a kind of gleam in her eyes that made him wary. "What are you planning?"

Her eyes widened as she gave him an innocent look, but he did not buy it for one second.

"Fine." She let out a little huff. "Eileen Bentley is in Miami. I can talk to her in person."

He scrubbed a hand over his face. "You're trying to put me in an early grave."

"Look, she's the last person I saw before that guy broke into my house."

"Julian already talked to her," he said. "He interviewed her thoroughly."

"Talking to her again won't hurt," Julian said from his desk, which was pushed up right against Carson's. "She was nice enough but not overly talkative. I feel like she might've been holding back. Not about her attorney's murder or anything, but maybe something to do with her husband?" He shrugged as he fixed his attention on Sienna. "If you get anything useful, let me know."

Sienna looked positively smug as she smiled at Carson. "See? You can keep me safe *and* we can get some work done too. It's a win-win."

He shot a look at Julian, who just lifted a shoulder.

"Let's get you packed and get out of here," he finally said. He wasn't letting her go see anyone when they were in Miami, but that was an argument he'd face once they got there. Sienna was just going to have to let his people do their jobs.

To his surprise, Sienna linked her arm through his as they headed out of the station.

Ah, hell. How was he going to keep his hands off her in Miami?

* * *

"So why don't you work for your brother?" Carson asked as they headed down the highway. After packing and tying up a few loose ends, they'd gotten on the road. The drive would be over five hours, but with Miami traffic, probably longer. But the farther they could get away from here, the better.

"I don't think I'd make a very good security professional."

He snorted softly. "Don't be a smart-ass. Not for Brodie. Why not work for Daniel doing what you do now? Just in a corporate angle."

"He's offered me a job a few times."

"No kidding. That's why I'm asking. Kathryn told me he's offered you a job at least once a month and you always turn him down."

"He told Kathryn that?"

"Of course. He wants you working for him. Why wouldn't he? You're smart and driven." He'd never worked with her personally, but he knew she'd assisted the PD on a few cases and everyone had great things to say about her. "Imagine how much good you could do with all of his resources. Right now you're basically a one-woman show... You know what, never mind. You'd probably take over the world if you started working for him."

She let out a low laugh, the throaty sound going straight to his dick. He rolled his shoulders once. Being in close quarters with her was wreaking havoc on him.

"What about you, you plan on being a detective forever?"

"I don't know, honestly. Right now I like it. I've got a good captain, but work life is long and I don't like the thought of locking myself in to one job forever." Something he'd never told anyone before.

"So how is it having Daniel as a brother-in-law?" she asked slyly.

He laughed lightly. "I never had a problem with Daniel. Okay, for the most part I didn't. Not until I thought he screwed up with my sister. But he treats Kathryn well and I see the way he looks at her." Daniel would never hurt her, not intentionally anyway. The man worshiped the ground Kathryn walked on.

"I know, right? They're kind of disgusting and I say that in the nicest way possible."

He laughed, liking this easy camaraderie with her. Sienna challenged him, but at the same time, things were so easy between them. He wished... Hell, he wished a lot of things. Like he could figure this woman out. Figure out how to get her back in his life in a way that didn't involve an investigation.

"Shit!" she yelped just as a big semi swerved in front of them.

Grasping the wheel, he jerked to the left to avoid a collision. His gaze snapped to the right, then left side mirror. Lines of cars were in both lanes behind them. *Hell.* He couldn't avoid it.

When the semi jerked wildly, its back end fishtailing, he winced and veered into the next lane of traffic. It was either that or a head-on collision.

Horns honked as the semi hit a truck's back end.

Gripping the wheel tight, he cut off a car, went flying into the median even as he pressed on the brakes. *Damn it!* He twisted at the last second, his side taking the brunt of the impact as they rammed into the guardrail.

The impact rattled through the vehicle, the airbags popping out with a whoosh.

They shuddered to a stop as the semi plowed ahead, crashing straight over the guardrail and smashing into the ditch between the opposite sides of the highway. Smoke billowed out from under the hood, a wild plume of it.

Cars behind them had all slammed on their brakes but it was a miracle no one had hit them from behind.

"Are you okay?" Trying to shove the airbag out of the way, he looked Sienna over.

"I'm good. How about you?" She looked him up and down too, scanning for any injuries.

"I'm fine." But his truck wasn't. Smoke was billowing out from under the hood too and when he tried to start it, the engine didn't turn over.

"I don't think we're making it to Miami tonight," she murmured.

Yeah, he didn't either.

CHAPTER NINE

"Just get in your bed," Sienna said in a grumpy tone.

Carson glanced over from the hotel window, let the curtain fall back into place. After the accident, they'd had to wait for the scene to be cleared, to deal with insurance, to make a report and then get a ride to the rental place. His truck was being towed back home to his normal mechanic, and right about now he was glad for insurance because they'd made things as easy as possible. Instead of driving into Miami tonight, they'd opted to grab dinner and stay in the nearest decent hotel.

But he couldn't stop pacing, couldn't stop looking out the window. "I don't like that our plans have been derailed." It had truly been an accident, but all the same, things had changed and an uneasy sensation had settled in his bones.

"I know. And we can just leave now if you want." She was sitting up in one of the two queen beds, her laptop on her lap.

"No. We're both exhausted." He stretched out on the bed parallel to hers, knowing he wasn't going to sleep well, but he didn't want to make her endure the rest of the drive this late at night. They both needed rest.

She closed her laptop and tucked it into her duffel bag. In yoga pants and a T-shirt, she had her hair down, literally and figuratively. He liked that she was just herself with him. That was one of the sexiest things about her.

"You want to watch TV, or just crash?" she asked as she got under the white sheets and flopped down on the pillow.

He'd rather be naked with her right now. "I'm fine either way."

"Okay. I'd rather not watch TV." She turned off the little lamp and lay back down.

He stared at the ceiling, painfully aware of his breathing and hers. Even with the outside traffic and muted noise, every shift against the sheet seemed overpronounced in the room. He'd imagined being in his bedroom with her—her bedroom. Any bedroom. But in those fantasies, they hadn't been clothed and in separate beds.

"Would you really be okay with me going into dangerous situations for my job?" Sienna suddenly asked into the dimness.

Her question startled him. The lights from the parking lot streamed in through the tiny gap between the curtains so he could see her well. "What?"

"I'm just curious. I want to know if you'd really be okay with me going into dangerous situations."

He paused as he tried to formulate his answer even as it registered that since she was asking, she'd been thinking about the possibility of being with him.

Apparently he didn't answer fast enough because she said, "See? This is why it would never work between us."

Oh, hell no. "Can you give me a second to give you an honest answer?" Without waiting for her to respond, he slid out of his bed and moved into hers.

She made a little yelp of surprise but didn't tell him to get back to his bed.

Lying on his side, he studied her as she turned to face him. She propped her head up on her hand, her eyes bright in the darkness and her dark hair spilling around her shoulders.

It was impossible not to be physically affected by her. And in this moment, he knew things could change between them. This was the opening he'd been waiting for. "I'm not going to *like* you going into dangerous situations. But I'm never going to tell you what to do with your life. For the most part I understand your job can be kind of boring, but that sometimes you get into sticky situations. Again, I'm not going to love that aspect. But I'm also not going to ask you to quit your job, because that would be like you asking me to quit mine."

She bit her bottom lip, watching him carefully. Her subtle vanilla scent teased the air, making him crazy.

"What about you? How do you feel about my job?" For the most part he got sent to calls where people were already dead or crimes had already been committed. So he was there for the aftermath. But he still faced dangerous situations on occasion. There was no way around that.

"I would never ask you to quit your job either, but...I'm not going to love that you're in danger." Then she bit her bottom lip again and he could see the wheels turning inside her head, and wished he knew exactly what she was thinking.

Taking a chance, he reached out and wrapped his fingers around her hip, flexed once. He liked holding her, however and whenever she would let him.

She let out a sort of sigh and leaned closer to him, erasing most of the distance. Not quite all of it, but this was very, very good.

He shifted a little closer, all the muscles in his body pulled tight as he erased the distance between them. She was finally opening up to him, actually talking about *them*. He wanted her so damn bad he ached.

To his relief, she slid her hands up his chest and clutched onto his shoulders as she pulled her body flush with his, erasing the final inches between them. And this was what he'd been waiting for, aching for.

They watched each other for a long moment, and when her gaze fell to his mouth he slanted his lips over hers, desperate for a taste of her. He'd been fantasizing about her for months. Hell, longer than that. Since pretty much the moment he'd seen her. Then he'd gotten to know her and it had been over for him.

As he delved his tongue into her mouth, she immediately threw a leg over his hip.

The two of them together had always been like fireworks going off. It was pure combustion. He forgot to think, sometimes forgot to breathe—like right now as she molded her long, lean body to his.

She tried to take over and push him onto his back, but he was balancing on a razor-thin wire, all his muscles bowstring tight, so he pinned her beneath him. He savored the feel of her under him, holding on to him, moaning into his mouth.

God, he'd missed her, missed this.

She arched against him, her breasts rubbing against his chest. Only two layers of material separated them, her T-shirt and his.

As they kissed, he slid his hands under her top, his fingers skating along her soft, smooth skin.

His cock was heavy between them, a desperate throb against his jogging pants. This was not how he'd imagined their day ending. Not even close. But Sienna underneath him, and—

A car alarm started blaring, obnoxiously loud as it sliced through the quiet.

He jolted, coming back to reality as he pulled back slightly. Breathing heavily, he looked down at her.

Sienna's lips were swollen, her eyes dilated as she looked up at him. "Ignore it," she rasped out, her fingers digging into his shoulders.

He wanted to. Oh, how he wanted to. But some kind of instinct had him moving, forcing himself off her even though leaving her warm, welcoming embrace was the last thing he wanted to do. "Give me a second," he murmured.

Returning to the window, he ignored his uncomfortable erection as he eased the curtain back.

The alarm was still blaring as he scanned the parking lot. A car near the front of the hotel was the culprit, its lights flashing in tune to the alarm. Stupid cockblock car alarm.

He started to step back, but paused as something in his hindbrain registered. Something...was off. He wasn't sure what it was though.

There. One of the security lights had gone out. No, *three* were out on the big light poles across the parking lot. And they hadn't been out when they'd arrived. He'd specifically picked a well-lit spot but the three out created a sort of triangle around their rental.

The back of his neck tingled with awareness, and when he turned around Sienna was sitting up, watching him carefully. "What is it?"

"Grab your stuff."

She didn't even question him, simply grabbed her sneakers and slipped them on before tugging a hoodie on over her top.

Neither of them had unpacked their clothes or toiletries since they'd only planned to stay the night. They each picked up their bag and instead of going out the door into the hallway, he opened the door to the neighboring room.

Normally each door would be locked, but as a precaution he'd rented two rooms next to each other, the second room under a different name—courtesy of one of Sienna's brothers.

As he shut the door to the neighboring room behind them, he flipped the lock into place.

"Should we leave?" she whispered.

He shook his head and held his finger to his mouth. Then he headed to the front door, glancing out the peep-hole.

Nothing.

He was probably being paranoid but he didn't care. Not when it came to Sienna's safety. He checked the window again. The car alarm had gone quiet now and even though there was faint street noise and a couple cars pulling into the hotel parking lot, it was quiet enough.

As he stepped back from the window, he heard the door of the room they'd just left slide open.

Sienna stiffened.

Carson grabbed his service weapon and pointed that they should hide in the little alcove where the bath-room was.

On silent feet they both moved in near silence, not turning any lights on.

There was a slight shuffling next door, maybe the sound of the bathroom door opening, and five long minutes later the main door into the hallway opened once more.

Motioning for her to stay where she was, Carson peered out the peephole again and saw a nondescript-looking white guy pull a hoodie over his head as he hurried down the hallway.

He counted to sixty then eased the door open. He kept his weapon down, out of sight, and after a glance in the hallway, he motioned for her to grab their bags.

He kept his hand on his weapon as they raced down the hallway in the opposite direction, hurrying toward the set of stairs instead of the elevators.

Once they were in the stairwell, he said, "We need to take the batteries out of our phones."

She'd already switched phones and no one was supposed to know she was with him, but someone had tracked them somehow. And he was betting on their phones being the easiest way.

After they'd done that, they quietly hurried down the rest of the stairs. Leaving in the rental car was out of the question. As soon as they exited downstairs, he glanced around the hallway, knowing they were momentarily exposed. He had his weapon tucked beneath his shirt but he didn't like any of this.

Somehow someone had found them despite all their precautions.

Instead of heading toward the lobby and going out the front doors, they went to a side exit.

"We need to get the video surveillance. And I have a backup burner phone we can use," Sienna murmured as they reached the exit doors. "I want to call my brother. Daniel will be able to get us out of here. Or get us a car. It's better than depending on a lift service company which will be linked to one of our credit cards." Technically they could use cash, but he wasn't even sure a driver would take them all the way to Miami on the promise of cash. No, they needed their own wheels.

And they'd have to turn their damn phones back on to contact a company. Even though Carson didn't like depending on her brother for anything, he nodded and quickly scanned the side of the hotel as they stepped out into the late-night air.

Cars zooming by on the nearby main road were louder here, the scent of exhaust filling the air. A row of hedges stood between them and the neighboring gas station.

"Give me your phone," he murmured.

Without question she handed it and the battery to him.

They moved to the row of hedges, and after ordering her to sit tight he made his way to the gas station parking lot. He pieced the phone together, took out the SIM and tossed it into the back of a pickup truck before casually heading into the gas station itself.

Right off the main highway, the place was busy, so he once again scanned the parking lot, looking for the man he'd seen. Nothing. Whoever had broken into their hotel room was likely long gone or trying to track their phones.

Hurrying back out, he met up with Sienna, who was still hidden in between hedges, tucked away out of sight. Her burner phone was in hand.

"What did your brother say?"

"He's got a rental for us. We can just make the drive to Miami tonight and hole up." She chewed on her bottom lip as she glanced around and he wanted to brush his fingers over her forehead, to smooth out the worry lines.

"How far is the rental place?"

"Not even a mile." They could easily walk that.

"Let's go, then." He'd worry about his rental car in the hotel parking lot later. For now, they needed to get the hell out of here.

CHAPTER TEN

"So what did Julian say?" Sienna asked as Carson strode into the living room overlooking the Atlantic.

They'd arrived an hour ago and had settled into the Miami condo—courtesy of her brother Daniel. No one except him—and Daniel's friend who owned this place—knew where they were, which was the point.

She was all out of sorts, had barely gotten any sleep, couldn't stop thinking about that kiss she and Carson had shared, and now she couldn't get in touch with her client, Eileen Bentley. Sienna had wanted to talk to her, especially after what had happened at the hotel hours ago. It was mid-morning so Eileen should definitely be awake.

"They got the security feed but weren't able to get anything off it. The guy must have used some kind of program because it wasn't just him avoiding cameras, there were blank spaces. They also found a tracking device on my rental car."

So…whoever had done this was a pro. That ball in her stomach hardened even more. And her worry over Eileen was now simmering. Sienna stood and walked to the sliding glass door, and stared out at the glittering blue water and white sand beaches. Everything in front of her was peaceful and soothing, but nothing could soothe her edges now. "I can't get a hold of Eileen." She ran her hand over her braid once as she turned back to him.

Her whole body was humming with energy and she didn't know if she should down more coffee or try to get in a couple hours of sleep. They needed to lie low but she desperately wanted to talk to Eileen in person. There were some things that you could see and judge in person as opposed to talking to someone over the phone. Though that was a moot point now, since Sienna couldn't even get in touch with her.

"You said she was coming down here to get away. There's no reason to think that she's in danger."

She lifted an eyebrow.

"Okay, there is. I just don't like you worrying." Carson glanced at her open laptop, frowned. "What's all this?"

"All the pictures I've taken in the last six months. I know it's like searching for a needle in a stack of needles, but I decided to rescan all of them. Maybe...I don't know, maybe there's something in one of the pictures that matters?" She was just working blind at this point. "I feel like I need to be doing more, I guess." She'd left her laptop in airplane mode so it wasn't connected to the internet. Not that she thought anyone had tracked her using her laptop. That took a special type of skill.

But Carson frowned, sat in front of her laptop and pulled up the photos she'd taken from the yacht. "Who are these men?"

"You already know that this is Wesley Bentley, Eileen's husband." She'd sent a solo picture of him to Julian and Carson for their files. "I figured I'd move backward through the pictures, starting with the most recent." She touched the screen above Bentley's face. "And that's his lawyer. But I don't know who this other guy is with them. I thought you saw them at the marina?"

Carson shook his head. "I never saw their faces, just their backs as they got on the boat."

"What's wrong, then?" Because his jaw had tightened slightly and he'd gone sort of still in the way he did when he was mulling something over. It was so damn sexy.

"Nothing. Did you send all of these to Julian?"

She shook her head. "There are a lot of pictures in there that...I'm not handing over to the police."

"Why not?"

"You *know* why not. A lot of those photos are people in compromising situations, and while they're using them during their divorces, if any of those photos become part of evidence, then they become public record. I don't like the idea of that, and you guys don't have a warrant." Because most of the cases she worked on, couples ended up coming to an agreement and settling before going in front of a judge. That way none of those pictures became public record.

His frown deepened, but he said, "Can you send me this picture? This guy looks familiar. I want to run him through our databases."

"That's fine. And if there are any other pictures that don't involve people in states of undress, I can provide those too. At least on a limited basis. Why don't you just send them to yourself?"

"Thanks." He got to work on her laptop while she went to the kitchen and ended up making herbal tea instead of coffee. Because the thought of more caffeine had her heart racing, and not in a good way.

"I think I might try and get a couple hours of sleep," she said as she returned to the living room. "My system is all messed up. Unless I need to be doing anything else right now?" She could keep looking at pictures but she'd been starting to lose focus each second that passed.

"No problem. I might grab some sleep too." He started to get up and then paused before clicking on something. Then he looked at her, his expression...strange.

"What?" She stepped forward to see what he'd pulled up. Immediately her cheeks flushed hot. *Oops.*

"You have pictures of us?"

"Kathryn sent me some wedding pictures." Dang it, why did she have to sound so defensive?

"These seem to be only pictures of me and you from the wedding." His voice had dropped an octave, his expression heated.

She could feel her cheeks flushing even warmer as she fought embarrassment. She had a few images with her and her brothers and her parents, but yep, she had a whoooole lot of her and Carson. Could the world open up and devour her now, please? "Why wouldn't I have them? I look amazing in that dress."

He stood then, his eyes heated as he moved in on her like a predator stalking its prey.

She very much wanted to be caught, however.

"You did look amazing in that dress. And I desperately wanted to get you out of it that entire night."

She'd had a little bit too much to drink that night, though she'd had a lot of fun with him. And she'd asked him up to her hotel room but he'd said no because of that very fact—that she'd had too much to drink. He'd been adamant that he would never take advantage of her. Which had just made her like him even more. She set her steaming tea on the nearest flat surface as she took another step back.

She wasn't sure where she was going or why she was even moving away from him. She wanted this man with every fiber of herself.

He kept coming, a strong, lethal panther ready to pounce.

"Carson," she whispered, not sure where she was going with that. He had her all twisted up inside, and had since the moment they'd first kissed. He made her feel things she'd never experienced, made her think about settling down. Something she'd never considered before.

He seemed so perfect and that alone terrified her. Her brothers had their lives together, seemed to be so adept at handling life in general. Whereas she was a mess on the best of days and Carson seemed to have this whole adulting thing down to an art. When they'd been at the hotel a few hours ago and she'd been internally panicking, he hadn't even broken a sweat. He'd just taken charge, and that was insanely hot.

"I think it's a good idea if we *both* grab a couple hours of sleep," he murmured as he reached her, those big, sexy hands settling on her hips in the most possessive way.

She bit back a groan. Damn, but she loved his possessive streak. The sun streamed in from the sliding glass doors and wall of windows behind him. He looked like a sexy warrior from another time, with broad shoulders, scruff on his face, and the light highlighting him from behind. But it was his eyes that drew her in, snared her.

"Just sleep?" Damn it, why was her voice all raspy and unsteady?

"Later." His gaze fell to her mouth, his blue eyes flaring wild and scorching hot. "I'm still clean...haven't been with anyone since you."

"Me neither. And I'm still on the pill." They'd talked about protection months ago and nothing had changed for either of them thankfully. If he'd been with someone else...well, it would have sucked. So knowing that he hadn't eased something inside her. Freed her.

Just like always, she swore she felt the sparks arcing between them.

She wasn't sure who moved first, him or her. But suddenly she had her legs wrapped around his waist and he had her pinned up against the nearest wall, his thick cock pressing into her.

His mouth ate at hers even as he rocked his hips into her.

Heat flooded her system as she arched into him. She wished they were already naked, that they'd already gotten to that part where no clothing separated them. She didn't want to think, she just wanted to feel, to experience all of Carson. To be consumed by him.

"Too many clothes." She might have said that out loud, she wasn't sure, but he pulled back and tugged her shirt off.

Next went her bra before his mouth descended on one of her already hard nipples. Her entire body was on fire for him, a live wire, pulsing and needy.

She groaned, digging her fingers into his shirt even as she tugged at it, desperate to get it off him.

For one moment, as he leaned back so she could strip him, she mourned the loss of his mouth on her body. But as soon as she tossed his shirt to the ground, he sucked her other nipple into his mouth.

She arched her back again, wanting more of this. More of him.

He playfully bit down, sending ribbons of pleasure straight to her clit. She was lightheaded and it had nothing to do with lack of sleep and everything to do with Carson.

Broad-shouldered, tall and sexy, he had this code of honor that she respected. And he was here with her, keeping her safe when she knew the department could have easily assigned someone else to this job.

He was here because he wanted her, had been pursuing her for months.

She was tired of fighting her attraction, tired of blaming him for the actions of former lovers. Tired of pretending that she was just fine being alone. She was, but she wanted more. She wanted Carson in her life. And not just for a night or two. Because Carson was like no one she'd ever known. He treated her like an equal, wasn't intimidated by her.

"Wall or bed?" he suddenly asked as he lifted his head to look at her.

She blinked, taking a moment to digest his question. The wall or bed? Wait... *Oh.* Then she understood. The wall sounded reeeeeally hot, but... "Bed." She wanted more room to taste all of him.

He clutched her ass and hauled her to the nearest bedroom. The curtains were open, with light spilling in over the airy comforter.

Moving quickly, he pinned her to the bed, the air of the comforter going out with a whoosh under the impact of their bodies.

"Pants off," she demanded before he could kiss her again and she lost all her senses. Because he had far too much clothing on and she'd been patient enough.

He grinned at her then, the action almost boyish and softening his features. "Mine or yours?"

"Both."

He groaned and tugged his pants off first. That was when she realized he went commando and her mouth watered. Like freaking Pavlov's dog. Holy hell, he was thick and perfect and her inner walls tightened as she stared for a long second.

She sat up and reached for him, wanting to stroke him with her fingers, wanting to feel that thickness, but he moved her hand out of the way as he grabbed her pants and panties off in one swoop. Maybe she'd start going commando too.

"Hell yes," he growled before he crawled onto the bed and covered her mouth with his even as he cupped her mound.

She wasn't even sure what the "hell yes" was for, but she didn't care. He was cupping her, rubbing his fingers against her slick folds, making her absolutely crazy. She rolled her hips against his hand, needy for more.

"Gotta taste you." It came out as a desperate groan before he started kissing his way down her body, setting her on fire with his mouth until he was between her legs, growling against her clit, his tongue wicked and wild and everything she remembered.

He slid two fingers inside her, curved them up in just the right angle as he started teasing her mercilessly with his tongue. She rolled her hips against his flicks and caresses, barely able to breathe for the pleasure shooting through her.

She was so damn close, so close to orgasm and she desperately wanted him inside her first. They'd been building up to this for months, even if she didn't want to admit it. Which, she didn't care anymore. She wanted all of him. Needed all of him like she needed her next breath.

"I want to..." Before she could finish, an orgasm punched through her fast and hard. Pleasure spiraled out to all of her nerve endings until she was a trembling mess against the comforter, her arms and legs jelly.

He looked up the length of her body, but didn't look smug. No, he still looked hungry.

Carson crushed his mouth to hers even as she reached between their bodies. She started stroking him as she guided him to her body. Not that he needed the help. He was primed and ready to go.

Far too slowly he pressed himself against her slick folds and just...teased her. He sort of pulsed there, just pushing the tip in and out and driving her crazy.

Not known for her patience, she rolled her hips upward, sucking in a breath as he completely filled her.

He growled against her mouth and started thrusting inside her.

She loved the sensation of being filled by him and was cursing herself for keeping her distance from him. For putting up walls and shutting him out.

She wasn't sure how long he thrust inside her, how long they met each other stroke for stroke. But she knew the moment he was going to come because his entire body went rigid above her. All his muscles went taut, his tattoos flexing with it.

But he seemed determined to make her come again as he reached between their bodies and started stroking her clit.

She hadn't thought she was capable of another orgasm but being filled completely by him, after fantasizing about him—them together—for months, she fell over the edge again, pleasure punching through her, taking over every last thought.

As soon as she did, he let go, coming inside her as he growled against her mouth. Time seemed to go still as they both climaxed, until they collapsed on the bed in a heap of pleasure.

Smiling up at him, she cupped his cheek, wanting to savor every second of this. The way he watched her, stared down at her, sort of awed her, leaving her speechless.

"Be right back," he murmured, suddenly disappearing.

Before she could mourn the loss of his warmth and presence he was back with a washcloth, his steady hand between her legs.

She...had to bite back a sudden bolt of emotion. Tears threatened at how gentle he was being, combined with everything they'd been through. And she knew she shouldn't be surprised but damn. This man was going to completely undo her.

"Shit," Carson suddenly cursed, setting the cloth down.

That was when she heard the ringing sound. What the hell was that? Her brain was all hazy, and as she tried to figure it out Carson eased off the bed.

"I've gotta grab that. It could be a development in the case."

Oh, his *phone*. She hurried after him, ignoring the stickiness between her thighs as she raced from the room, not bothering with clothing.

"Yeah," he said into his phone. He swore softly. Then there was a whole lot of silence and though his expression barely changed, there was a flicker of surprise in his eyes. "What does this mean for us?"

Sienna stood close to him, wishing she could hear whoever was on the other end.

He reached for her, pulling her close against him and she pressed her body flush against his. He was this big, soothing wall of steadiness. Everything about him was real and dependable. And in the past she would've thought those qualities weren't sexy, but she liked that she could depend on him. That he meant what he said.

That he always had her back. Even though it meant she was falling way too hard for this man. A man who could very easily break her heart.

"Okay, just send me the information," he said quietly. "We're not going anywhere. The place has enough food for a few days, so we'll just hang tight."

"What is it?" she demanded as soon as he ended the call.

In response he brushed his mouth over hers, then tried to deepen his kiss, but she pinched his side as they stood there naked in the middle of the living room.

The way he watched her had her toes curling against the tile. "That was incredible. You're incredible," he added. Then his expression sobered. "That was Julian," he said as he guided them back to the bedroom.

He grabbed his jeans and tugged them on as she sat on the end of the bed. "That guy in the picture with your client's soon-to-be ex-husband and attorney? The unknown man is Graham Jordan. He's bad news. Apparently the Feds had him under investigation for money laundering and a whole list of other crap. It sounds like they wanted to turn him against his boss, who is also bad news, but doesn't concern us in this situation. They'd been building a case against him, and had been planning to bring Jordan in when he 'died.'"

"But...Jordan's not dead, right?" Obviously not, if she'd just taken a picture of him.

"Nope. So we have strict instructions to sit tight."

"That's it?" She grabbed the blanket on the end of the bed and wrapped it around her.

"This is in the Feds' hands now. They're looking for Jordan and believe he targeted you because you took those photographs of him. He was friends with Wesley, or business associates I should say. The Feds believe he was tying up loose ends with you and Eileen's lawyer since you both saw those pictures."

Sienna nodded slowly. "What about Kevin Fox, then? He had nothing to do with the Bentleys."

Carson shrugged, seemingly unconcerned.

"That's all I get? A shrug?"

"Look, I'm *not* unconcerned. I'm very concerned about your safety, in fact. And that is my only priority. Julian's very good at what he does. And part of me wishes I was with him, working on this case right now, but I would much rather be with you, making sure you are safe. They'll figure things out, and with the FBI's resources they'll find Graham Jordan."

Well when he put it that way, he warmed her from the inside out.

"They also think Wesley Bentley is dead as well," he added.

She blinked. "Wait, what?"

"Yep." He sat on the bed, pulled her onto his lap. "They found a lot of blood at his house. And it's definitely his—they've already tested it."

"My head kind of hurts with what this might mean." She continued talking as she worked through everything. "So, if he's dead, it means there's definitely no divorce. And no way those pictures become public record. But why not go after Eileen instead of Wesley to make sure there was no divorce?"

"Maybe getting to Wesley was easier, more convenient. With Wesley dead, there's definitely no divorce, and no need for anyone to get their hands on those pictures now. That said..." He cleared his throat, looking as if he didn't want to continue. "She might still be in danger. She's seen the pictures. Even if she doesn't know who Jordan is, he might not want to take the chance that she recognizes him."

And Sienna had taken the pictures. No wonder someone had broken into her house, stolen her electronics. Too bad for them, they'd grabbed the wrong stuff. "So what does this mean for me?"

"We sit tight. That's it."

Gah. Not the answer she wanted, but she knew it was all she was getting for now. As she digested this new information, she leaned into him, resting her head on his shoulder. "I'm glad I'm here with you," she murmured. "I mean, I'm not glad about the circumstances."

"So I'm not just a way to pass the time?" There was a surprising hint of vulnerability in his voice.

She lifted her head to look at him, saw that same vulnerability mirrored in his gaze. "Definitely not. If I had to be with someone else through all this, there's no one I'd rather be with than you," she said, meaning it—right before she kissed him.

CHAPTER ELEVEN

"I've never seen you like this." Carson's voice was carefully neutral as he looked over at Sienna by the window.

"I don't like being cooped up like this." When she got cooped up without a purpose, she started to pace. It helped expel her energy. They'd had lots of sex last night, then again this morning, and then they'd done an actual workout in the living room. But she was still keyed up.

"We've been here *one* night." Now his tone was dry as he looked up from his laptop. Every fifteen minutes or so he would get down on the ground and do sit ups or push-ups, keeping his body moving. So he really wasn't that much different than her.

She just got more visibly antsy, apparently. "Yeah, and I hate it. I mean, I don't hate being here with you, I just don't like feeling useless. And I can't find any more about Kevin Fox. I don't know how he ties into all this and it's bugging me." At least his wife Hailey was still in Canada.

Carson had started to respond when his phone rang. "Yeah?" he answered.

She recognized the ringtone and knew it was his partner.

Carson said a handful of "yeahs" mixed in with grunts that could have meant anything. Then his expression darkened slightly before he ended the call.

"They found the guy?"

"No. Julian is in town. He's with the lead agent on the case tasked with hunting down Jordan."

"They're here in Miami?"

"Yeah."

"So why do you look like your cat died?"

"I can think of a few reasons why they're here—and want to see us. You specifically."

"Me? They said that?"

"Yeah. The Fed brought Julian along and my partner didn't say much on the phone—probably because he knows I'm not going to like what they have to say."

"What do you think they're going to say?"

He scrubbed a hand over his face and looked away from her, out the window. "I don't want to speculate, but they'll be here in an hour. Do you want to change or something?" His gaze flicked back to her, appreciation in his blue eyes as they swept over her little shorts and sports bra.

"Change? Like what, into a frog?"

He snorted. "You know what I meant."

"What's wrong with my outfit?"

His jaw clenched slightly and she suppressed a laugh. She wasn't actually going to wear this to meet some federal agent, but she liked messing with him a bit. "I mean, I guess I can take my panties off underneath the shorts? Would you like that?"

He barked out a laugh even as he stood and basically stalked her across the room. "I'm going to take them off right now."

"That better be a promise."

* * *

Sienna couldn't stop the nervous energy humming through her as Carson let his partner and the woman with him into the condo. Definitely a federal agent.

Both Julian and the woman scanned the place in the way those in law enforcement did. They swept everything with a critical eye before Julian introduced them. "This is Special Agent Annie Collins." He indicated the petite redhead in the dark blue pantsuit and killer heels.

Carson shook her hand once before Sienna did the same, except Sienna actually smiled, whereas Carson looked all surly.

The woman returned her smile and it looked genuine. Sienna was good at reading people—it was why she did so well at her job. So at least they were off to a good start.

Carson gestured that they should all sit in the open living room. The living area and kitchen in this condo were connected, so it felt a whole lot bigger than it actually was.

"You're not using Sienna as bait," Carson said into the quiet of the room, even though his body language screamed *don't screw with me* as he sat right next to Sienna.

And wrapped a possessive arm around her shoulders.

She was surprised by the possessive display as much as by what he'd just said. They hadn't talked about how they were going to act with each other before his partner got here, but Carson was making his stance clear. Also, bait? What the heck was he talking about?

The federal agent looked mildly surprised as she glanced between the two of them then shot a look at Julian, who had an incredible poker face.

The other detective was about the same height as Sienna and had a similar runner's build. But he had bronze skin, giving him a sun-kissed glow, and probably used more hair products than she did. The times she'd seen him, he always looked so put together and now was no different.

"We're not going to use her as bait," Agent Collins said.

"Then why are you here?" Carson asked bluntly.

Normally Sienna would have a hundred questions but Carson was handling things perfectly so she was going to sit back and see what happened. For now anyway.

The woman cleared her throat once. "We currently have Eileen Bentley with us."

Sienna shoved out a breath. So that was why she couldn't get a hold of her client. Which was better than what she'd been imagining. "Is Eileen okay?"

"She is. She's stressed that her soon-to-be ex-husband was killed, and that it's very likely tied to their divorce proceedings. She's worried about you, but she's hanging in there."

"Good."

"What we want from you is simple. We just want you to make a phone call to her. We have a feeling we know who Graham Jordan hired to come after you—the man we think killed Bentley as well as Valentina Hall."

"You don't think he's behind the murders himself?" Sienna asked because she simply couldn't help herself. She really did like puzzles and mysteries. But more than anything, she wanted justice for Valentina.

"No." Then the agent paused and seemed to weigh her next words. "At least not all of the murders. Jordan has gotten his hands dirty before so it's *possible* he's involved directly. Either way, definitely indirectly. We're going to catch him, it's just a matter of time."

Sienna nodded, watching her carefully. Since she didn't know anything about the agent, she was going to have to go on instinct with whether she trusted the other woman or not. Thankfully Carson's presence was soothing, and when he gently squeezed her shoulder, she leaned farther into him, savoring his warmth.

"Like I was saying," Agent Collins continued. "We just want you to make a phone call using a clone of your phone. We want our target to trace it to where Eileen is staying. We've got her set up in a safe house where we have eyes on her. We want to catch Jordan's hired guy in the act. He works for money so we think he'll flip on Jordan."

"What if Jordan comes himself?" Sienna asked.

"Then we take him down and get him to flip on the guy he hired."

"That's it? You just want me to make a phone call?" That seemed too easy.

"Yes. You guys were tracked to that hotel using electronics, that much we know. So it stands to reason that the man he hired has the skills to track Eileen as well. She's had her phone off, but he'll be monitoring, waiting to find her."

Sienna looked up at Carson. His jaw was clenched tight, but not as bad as before. "What do you think?" she asked.

He looked surprised, maybe that she'd asked him. "As long as you don't screw anything up," he said to Agent Collins, "then this is fine."

"We just want this to be authentic. We have a script for what we want Ms. MacArthur to say to Eileen. She's going to say she wants to meet up with Eileen—it won't really be her," she hurried out when Carson started to argue. "We've got a body double. We just need to get one of these men out in the open. From there we're confident we'll be able to bring both of them down with no more loss of life."

"They're really prepared," Julian added, looking pointedly at Carson. "They know what they're doing."

Sienna knew sometimes different law enforcement agencies didn't get along with each other, but it was pretty clear that Julian trusted the Feds. Or at least Agent Collins. If he did, then she was going to as well. "I'm in. I have no problem making a phone call. I want to bring down Valentina's killer. She was such a good person." A good mom. Sienna swallowed hard, pushing back the bubble of emotion that threatened to spill over. Now was definitely not the time.

"Okay, then. We're ready to do this now," Collins said. "I brought the clone with me. And I guarantee it won't be traced here to you. It'll ping off a nearby beach, making it look as if you called from a random stretch of white sand."

"Let's do this." The sooner the Feds caught these monsters, the sooner everyone could go back to their lives.

CHAPTER TWELVE

Sienna realized she was humming to herself as she scanned the takeout menu for the fancy barbecue restaurant at the bottom of this high-rise. Though fancy barbecue seemed like an oxymoron.

She didn't care that she was humming and acting like, well, like she'd never been this dang happy before. Because being with Carson made her ridiculously happy. She wondered if maybe it was just that the situation they were in was intense, but no, she'd wanted him long before this. And she knew he'd wanted her too.

After calling Eileen and playing her part in all this, they hadn't heard anything all day from Julian or the Feds and she was really, *really* trying not to stress out.

Sienna and Carson had of course had sex, then gone to the gym downstairs for an intense workout, and now Carson was in the shower. She'd insisted on him going first because she'd known he wouldn't let her actually shower if she joined him. Plus she'd needed to cool down.

Picking up her cell phone, she'd started to call the restaurant when a very faint click reached her ears.

She froze, her fight-or-flight instinct kicking in. That was the front door opening.

There was no way to get out of the kitchen without revealing herself—unless she jumped over the countertop. Because the exit from the small kitchen was right into the hallway—which would give whoever had just broken in a full view of her. And a chance to shoot her if they were carrying.

Dropping the menu from cold fingers, she scrambled over the countertop, trying to be as quiet as possible.

At this point, stealth be damned, she just needed to get to her weapon. Which she had stupidly left in the bedroom.

Her bare feet were quiet against the tile as she raced down the short adjoining hallway to their bedroom. She would only have seconds and she was too afraid to call out to Carson. No, she needed to get the pistol first.

She pulled the weapon from the top drawer of the only dresser and started to hurry into the bathroom to warn him, but froze when she heard soft footsteps on the tile behind her.

Moving quickly, she backed up against the wall and, using the mirror from the dresser, watched as a man wearing a long-sleeved black T-shirt and a balaclava over his face—weapon up—strode down the hallway.

Blood rushed in her ears but she kept her eyes pinned on the target. He couldn't have seen her yet.

She would only get one shot at this. And she had to make it count. She'd practiced shooting in a controlled environment but she'd never actually shot anyone before and could admit she was terrified.

As he drew nearer to the room, the shower stopped.

The gunman swept into the room, his body angled toward the open bathroom door.

Gripping the pistol tight, she felt as if she was having an out-of-body experience as she whipped around from behind the dresser, pistol up. "Drop your gun!" she screamed, way louder than she'd intended.

The man, with his weapon pointed directly into the bathroom, froze. His entire body was poised as he gave her the side-eye.

She could see it from his body language, no way was he dropping his weapon.

"Do it!" she shouted even as he started to turn toward her.

She fired on instinct. It was either him or her. Or Carson. Hell no!

Pop. Pop. Pop

Glass shattered as he shot at her, his body jerking back as her bullets made contact.

"Duck!" Carson shouted.

She listened, crouching and lowering her weapon as Carson slammed into the guy, tackling him to the ground.

She was barely aware of moving as she jumped over the bed, kicking the man's gun out of the way as Carson slammed his fist against the guy's jaw with a sickening thud.

The guy slumped, his whole body going limp under the assault.

In moments, Carson had the man facedown, his body pinned against the tile. He was holding the shooter's arms behind him at an angle that looked incredibly painful had the guy been conscious.

"Get my cuffs! Top drawer," he ordered.

With trembling fingers she managed to grab his silver cuffs and toss them to Carson. After that, everything happened so quickly. Carson called Julian, asking for backup.

She was trembling, blood rushing in her ears as she tried to keep it together, but in reality she could barely move from where she was rooted by the dresser.

"He has a vest on." Carson's voice ripped her out of her thoughts as she stared at the man on the ground who still hadn't moved since Carson punched him.

She blinked. "What?"

Carson placed his big hands on her shoulders, his eyes searching hers. "He has a vest. You didn't kill him. He might have some broken ribs—and maybe a broken jaw—but he'll live. Julian is on the way with an ambulance."

She wasn't sure why that mattered but for some reason it did. This guy had come here to kill both of them but still...she didn't want to be responsible for taking another's life.

Throat tight, she nodded. "You really need some pants," she whispered.

Carson looked stunned for a moment before he barked out a short laugh. "You're probably right."

CHAPTER THIRTEEN

Sienna wrapped her fingers around the mug of hot coffee even though it was late at night as she and Carson sat in the office of Special Agent Collins.

The local Fed station was a lot different than the police department back home. It was quiet here, the walls gray, and everyone was in suits even with the later hour. There was a decent amount of activity, but everyone seemed to work quieter.

"Thank you for everything you've done to help us," Agent Collins said, looking between the two of them.

They'd been brought in to make an official report—the Feds had originally separated them so they could make their statements—and Sienna just wanted to leave. But she nodded politely because she also wanted more details. "Can you tell us anything about that man or...I guess anything that happened with Eileen? Is she okay?"

The woman paused, then seemed to come to a decision. "The man who broke into your place is Miles Hunt. He was hired by Graham Jordan to help him eliminate anyone who'd seen the images of him. They've worked together in the past, so it isn't a surprise that's who he hired. But they've both already tried to flip on each other. They're both trying to make deals. Hunt swears he didn't kill your attorney friend. He says Graham did that himself and I tend to believe him. That kill was too messy, especially with the added arson. The others were much more professional and lined up with what we know about his alleged past. We've been after him for a while too."

"Did you know Hunt was going to come after Sienna?" There was an underlying edge to Carson's tone even though his body language was casual as he sat with her on the other side of the agent's desk.

"No. He..." She cleared her throat. "The phone we had her use was secure. He tracked your partner. Something we didn't consider since he was with me most of the time. But it's how Hunt found your location. That's on me and I apologize. The only consolation I can give you is that he won't be getting out of jail for a long time."

"Will we need to testify?" Sienna asked.

"Doubtful. He's working on a deal right now. He's got a lot of information not just on Jordan, but others. He's hopefully going to give it in exchange for no trial and a prison of his choice."

"Are either of us in danger?" Carson asked.

"No. There's no reason to come after either of you now. Sienna was just a contract to him. And he's going to be turning on a lot of former clients. If anything, he's in danger of..." She cleared her throat instead of continuing. "We have no reason to believe you're in danger anymore. You're free to go."

"Thanks." Carson stood before she'd finished speaking.

Sienna set her coffee on the desk and stood with him. "Oh...I know I've asked about this, but what about Kevin Fox? Was his death involved with—"

"It had nothing to do with this. From what we can tell, he was killed by someone he pissed off before he went to jail. At least that's what it's looking like according to the local police department. It was just a coincidence that he was one of your clients and got killed around the same time as the others."

Well there was that, then. Sienna's head hurt as they strode out the office door.

"You want to get a place for the night? Or head straight home?" Carson asked her.

It would be a decent drive up the coast of Florida but she wanted to be home, wanted to sleep in her own bed—with him. She wanted this whole mess behind them. "Home."

* * *

Carson grabbed Sienna's duffel bag from the back seat of the rental before they strode up the front walk to her house. The sun was just peeking above the horizon, illuminating everything in oranges and pinks. It was early enough yet that the humidity of the day hadn't set in and there was a decent breeze blowing through the trees.

They'd stopped at a diner to grab some food then driven straight here, and while Sienna had tried to sleep, she hadn't been able to get any. He left his bag in the rental car, unsure if she wanted him to stay or not. The drive home hadn't been awkward, but now that they were back to reality, he wondered if she was going to place him back in that box she'd kept him in before.

"I just remembered I need to call my brother and tell him about his friend's condo." She sighed softly.

"Daniel isn't going to care. He'll just be happy that you're alive." So was Carson. When he'd heard her scream from the bedroom, telling that bastard to drop his weapon, it had shaved a decade off Carson's life. Punching the guy hadn't been enough. He was only sorry he hadn't actually broken the guy's jaw.

"True enough." She cleared her throat as they stood there on the porch. "Do you have to work today?"

"I...have no idea." He hadn't even talked to his boss. Julian had taken over everything, had told him to just call him when he got back to town.

It was Tuesday morning but he doubted his boss wanted him to come in, considering everything that had happened. Still, he would need to check in officially.

"This feels kind of weird to say, but even with everything that happened I still had fun with you. You know, when that guy wasn't shooting at us."

He snorted at her words and leaned down to brush his lips over hers.

"Do you want to come in, or...?" She left the question hanging in the air but the exhaustion on her face told him everything he needed to know—she just wanted to sleep.

Frustration slid through him even as disappointment joined in. He wasn't going to force himself into her home when she was just being polite. He'd made mistakes with her before and he didn't want to do that again. She'd just been through a lot, had shot someone. It didn't matter that the guy had been wearing a vest; she'd shot with the intention to kill. He shoved back all his possessiveness, shoved back the need to demand she let him stay. "No, but I'll call you. You need to get sleep and I've got to check in with my boss."

"Okay. Talk to you later, then." She wrapped her arms around him, giving him a hug then a quick kiss before hurrying inside her house, shutting and locking the door behind her.

The sound of the lock clicking into place made a weird sort of sensation settle in his bones.

As he walked back to the car, he couldn't stop the hollowness filling him. He didn't want to leave. He had the sudden thought that he wished they lived together, which was insane. But he wanted to wake up to her face every morning. Wished that right about now they were both crashing in a bed they owned together.

But it was way too soon to be thinking about that. Right?

CHAPTER FOURTEEN

Carson waited as long as he could. And maybe he should have given Sienna more than a few hours, but screw that.

He'd decided not to give her the chance to put walls up between them again. Hell, he never should have left earlier, but he'd been sleep-deprived and unsure of what to do about her.

Not anymore. Well, he was still sleep-deprived, but he didn't care. He knew exactly what he wanted.

When he pulled into her driveway, he saw both her brothers' vehicles there and gritted his teeth. He hadn't wanted to deal with her family right now, but it was what it was.

Moments after he knocked on the door, Daniel answered it, frowned at him. Brodie was right behind him, not exactly frowning, but...watching him intently.

"You don't need to answer the door!" Sienna called out from somewhere in the house, annoyance tingeing her voice. "I'm more than capable."

Her brothers ignored her.

"What are you doing here?" Daniel asked.

"Is everything okay?" Brodie continued.

"I'm here to see Sienna." He'd barely gotten the words out before Sienna appeared.

She was quickly followed by his own sister, Kathryn, who looked surprised to see him. But then she grinned almost knowingly.

"Can I talk to you? Alone?" he asked Sienna after giving Daniel a pointed look. Brodie was just hanging back by this point. Then Carson handed Daniel the coffee and bag of pastries he'd brought for Sienna. "And put these in her kitchen. Don't touch them. They're not for either of you."

"Someone is testy this morning," Kathryn murmured as Sienna stepped onto the front porch with him.

"Did something happen with the case?" she asked as she shut the door behind her.

In response, he cupped her face and slanted his mouth over hers. He'd definitely made a mistake leaving before. He should have taken her straight to bed and held her in his arms while they both crashed.

She moaned against him, leaning into his body as she kissed him back with a fierceness that matched his own hunger. Blinking, she finally looked up at him, her expression dazed. "Not that I'm complaining. At all. But what was that for?"

"I wanted to stay earlier. But I wasn't sure if you wanted me to, and for the first time that I can remember, I felt like a teenager, unsure of myself. And I don't want to leave things up in the air between us. I know I could've called but I wanted to see you in person. I'm in love with you, Sienna," he said bluntly, because it was the truth. "I let you put walls between us before and I'm not doing that ever again. Right now I'm laying it out there and letting you know that I want more than just dating you. I want to be exclusive. I want to be able to stay over. I want you to stay over at my place. I want you to take up half my closet or more if you want. I want to worry about you when you go off to work—"

She grabbed him by the front of his shirt and yanked him to her, kissing him hard and long. He wrapped her up in his arms, savoring every sweet kiss as he pressed her up against the front door.

"I love you too," she rasped out finally. "And I wanted you to stay earlier too, but I was sleep-deprived and you're *really* hard to read. I didn't want to be all needy and have you stay out of a sense of duty or whatever. But I'm so glad you're here now."

"I knew I should've stayed," he murmured, kissing her again.

The door flew open and Daniel glared at him. "Why don't you just come in here? It's better than making out on her front porch for the whole neighborhood to see."

Sienna simply rolled her eyes but wrapped her arm around Carson's waist as he tugged her close to him. "You better not have touched my pastries," she said, jabbing Daniel in the ribs with a light punch.

"I might've." He grinned, completely unrepentant.

Carson locked the door behind them, kissing her on the head as they strode toward the kitchen. He loved this woman and she loved him back.

It was almost too much to believe. Soon he was going to figure out a polite way to ask her brothers and his sister to leave. Or maybe he'd just forget being polite and tell them to get the hell out so he could have Sienna to himself.

EPILOGUE

Four months later

Carson held his wife in his arms—his wife, something he would never get tired of saying—as they danced at their wedding.

Her family had wanted longer to plan a wedding but that had been unnecessary, and Sienna hadn't cared one way or the other. So they'd settled on a December wedding, which meant he got to end this year as a man married to the woman of his dreams.

"What are you thinking about?" Sienna murmured, burrowing closer against him.

"Our honeymoon."

She threw her head back and laughed, the sound music to his ears. As always.

She was stunning today, no surprise. In her strapless white dress, her hair down in gorgeous waves, it had taken all his restraint not to thread his fingers through her thick tresses. But only because his sister had warned him that even though her hairstyle looked simple, he would mess everything up. Then Brodie's fiancée had threatened him with a curling iron—so he'd listened to the women.

But soon he was going to mess up Sienna's hair, strip her dress off and bury his face between her legs. Very, very soon.

"I have a feeling you're thinking something dirty for sure," she murmured before going up on her toes and kissing him.

"Maybe a little." He grinned against her mouth as the music played around them.

Both their families were there as well as a decent-sized crowd, but all of his focus was on her. The woman who had definitely made him a better man.

They'd been living with each other practically since the moment they got back from Miami, and while he sometimes worried about her at work, he knew she could take care of herself. He was honored to be married to such a strong, wonderful woman.

A smart-ass he would never let go.

—The End—

ACKNOWLEDGMENTS

Thank you to my usual crew; Kaylea Cross, Julia, Sarah and Jaycee! Critique partner, editor, assistant, and cover designer. You guys are wonderful and so appreciated. I'm also grateful to my readers. Thank you for reading another of my stories. And now that I've thanked my writer pups once, they're demanding to be in all my acknowledgments. So thank you to Piper and Jack, the two laziest, silliest pups a writer could ask for.

COMPLETE BOOKLIST

Ancients Rising Series

Ancient Protector

Ancient Enemy

Ancient Enforcer

Ancient Vendetta

Darkness Series

Darkness Awakened

Taste of Darkness

Beyond the Darkness

Hunted by Darkness

Into the Darkness

Saved by Darkness

Guardian of Darkness

Sentinel of Darkness

A Very Dragon Christmas

Darkness Rising

Deadly Ops Series

Targeted

Bound to Danger

Chasing Danger (novella)

Shattered Duty

Edge of Danger

A Covert Affair

Endgame Trilogy
Bishop's Knight
Bishop's Queen
Bishop's Endgame

MacArthur Family Series
Falling for Irish
Unintended Target
Saving Sienna

Moon Shifter Series
Alpha Instinct
Lover's Instinct
Primal Possession
Mating Instinct
His Untamed Desire
Avenger's Heat
Hunter Reborn
Protective Instinct
Dark Protector
A Mate for Christmas

O'Connor Family Series
Merry Christmas, Baby
Tease Me, Baby
It's Me Again, Baby
Mistletoe Me, Baby

Red Stone Security Series®
No One to Trust
Danger Next Door
Fatal Deception
Miami, Mistletoe & Murder
Continued...

Red Stone Security Series® continued...

His to Protect

Breaking Her Rules

Protecting His Witness

Sinful Seduction

Under His Protection

Deadly Fallout

Sworn to Protect

Secret Obsession

Love Thy Enemy

Dangerous Protector

Lethal Game

Secret Enemy

Saving Danger

Redemption Harbor Series®

Resurrection

Savage Rising

Dangerous Witness

Innocent Target

Hunting Danger

Covert Games

Chasing Vengeance

Sin City Series (the Serafina)

First Surrender

Sensual Surrender

Sweetest Surrender

Dangerous Surrender

Deadly Surrender

Verona Bay

Dark Memento

Deadly Past

Linked books

Retribution

Tempting Danger

Non-series Romantic Suspense

Running From the Past

Dangerous Secrets

Killer Secrets

Deadly Obsession

Danger in Paradise

His Secret Past

Paranormal Romance

Destined Mate

Protector's Mate

A Jaguar's Kiss

Tempting the Jaguar

Enemy Mine

Heart of the Jaguar

ABOUT THE AUTHOR

Katie Reus is the *New York Times* and *USA Today* bestselling author of the Red Stone Security series, the Darkness series and the Redemption Harbor series. She fell in love with romance at a young age thanks to books she pilfered from her mom's stash. Years later she loves reading romance almost as much as she loves writing it.

However, she didn't always know she wanted to be a writer. After changing majors many times, she finally graduated summa cum laude with a degree in psychology. Not long after that she discovered a new love. Writing. She now spends her days writing paranormal romance and sexy romantic suspense.

For more information on Katie please visit her website: www.katiereus.com.

Made in the USA
Las Vegas, NV
14 April 2021

21369173R00079